DANNAYE CARTER                    BOUTIQUE

PAPERBACK VERSION:
ISBN-13: 9780692023242
ISBN-10: 0692023240

I0517422

PUBLISHED BY: KENERLY PRESENTS-FAM CARTEL
COVER ART: AMB Branding and Design
Book Layout by FAM CARTEL/KENERLY PRESENTS
Editing by CHARNESE GRAHAM

To order additional copies of this book, contact:
FAM CARTEL-KENERLY PRESENTS
Follow me on Twitter @DK_Cartier
Facebook: Dannaye Carter

Interested in Author appearances, interviews, and other publications by Kenerly Presents Authors contact: Shaunta Kenerly via email at shauntakenerly@yahoo.com

1

# "THE BOUTIQUE"

As a successful entrepreneur I became exposed to an abundance of other entrepreneurs. We all shared the same common understanding; money was the object of focus. As a successful entrepreneur would say balance is key.  The skill to immediately cut off work at home and home at work was phenomenal to the hustle. Hustlers observed things in a different way and adjusted our game face.  Full force, work bitch. Direct and clear about her daily tasks and objectives. That's why it was easy for a woman like me to cut off my fellow nobles if they ever crossed me. It had to be done. If I held on to each situation that ever caused any hardship to my life, my whole damn operation would be in complete shambles. I was one of those people that had a hard time forgiving people for what they've done to me. I felt if you really cared about me, you wouldn't do anything to cross me. Shit like that became difficult to maintain, I worked around my sisters. Those hoes were always in my business. They called in the middle of everything. I could be in mid fuck, mid cum, they don't give a damn. They had an emergency and needed my ear at that very moment.

Coming up in the Streets of Columbus, we gained a lot of street knowledge. We all helped each other out some type of way. Out of the 6 women described in this circumstance three of us were sisters, two of us were blood related and our sister was the daughter of my mother's husband Raymond Carlson. Mr. Ray, our stepfather remarried our mother, and relocated to Chicago IL when we were three, five and seven.

My mother became the wife of one of the top nephrologist in Chicago IL. Mr. Ray had it made. He had his Mrs. on a tight leash and at his every call. My mother was a show off so I know she soaked up his cockiness, and swallowed it too if you will. She made sure she reaped every last benefit she could of being a doctor's wife. Except bearing one of his children. My mother only had Tinsley and I. She left my father when she was pregnant with Tinsley. My mother said that my dad starting using drugs and bringing the friends he was using with, to our house. My mother was very conservative and at the time working for a huge phone company and lived in the suburbs. My mother said that after leaving my father she didn't want any more children, but I knew better than that. I knew damn well she would have been more than ecstatic to have Mr. Ray's kids as well. She wasn't fooling anybody. She was still a bit insecure about Mia's mom Michelle, and her ass was clear across the country. Of course being a provider and prideful about finances, Mr. Ray still bought Mia's mother a house and car after getting full custody of Mia. My mother didn't understand the logic but, her friends and even my grandmother, filled her head with the bullshit.

"He's making sure she has stability all the way in Texas, simply because on his business trips he needs a home to go to," They would explain.

My mother should have been smarter than to believe those lies. Mr. Ray despised Mia's mother. He never spoke bad about her in front of Mia, but his body language said otherwise. He never encouraged Mia to call or even go see her for that matter. Mr. Ray was a private man. He typically moved alone. Mr. Ray was very conservative, and I strongly believed he didn't surround his self around messy situations such as going back to his ex-wife who divorced her child the same time she divorced her husband. He was smooth in every aspect. From the way he talked to the advice he gave us girls.  I don't think she should've believed other people who weren't even in relationships for themselves. They gave her headaches when she thought of the so-called helpful relationship advice. Late night girl talks only sent her straight to his Voice mails, and zoned completely out when he returned. Typically returning home on Sunday mornings, you could imagine how we spent our Sunday's. However, he kept bread at her table, so she indulged just to give her girls the world, she had more fun satisfying her own material wants, but it was all worth it when he became a primary provider for us. Mr. Ray was such a great example of money controlling an unjust situation. Although Mr. Ray wasn't my real father, He was the father figure in our life. He also took his parenting very serious.  The man that I would one day marry would be an example of Mr. Ray.

# SHALLOW HEARTS

"Dionne, honey, you're just like your father," My mother explained as I helped her cut up peppers in the kitchen.

"Mom, please. I hate when you bring him up, I barely know him so I wouldn't be able to agree," I interrupted as my mother began to tell me a story about my missing father.

I know He lived in Columbus, Oh and we've stumbled upon each other on numerous occasions. I still had contact with family members of his who made the effort to at least invite Tinsley and I to holiday events. When he saw us he would ask if either of us had any kids laugh, then rub our heads and pretty much disappear for long periods of time. We barley spoke of him; in fact we barely showed any emotion about the man. For all we knew Mr. Ray was a standing father for us, and we didn't know anyone else. My mother never spoke bad about him, not even my grandmother who had something to say about everybody. I think everyone was trying to erase him from their memory.

"I mean you are extremely stubborn. You need to think of hiring in other girls at Pearl who have prior retail experience," My mother suggested as she filled her casserole pan with ground meat, peppers and spaghetti sauce.

When it came to the boutique I was open to all the advice my mother and grandmother suggested. I held tight to their every word. When we first re-opened the boutique it had already made its mark in this city.  Our Boutique was legendary. My grandmother Cecelia Priss Ann Harris, or Me Me Priss as we would call her also known as Prissy Mae, had this city's fashion on complete lock in the 80's and 90's. I mean anybody that came through this city back then, stopped by my grandmother's boutique. My grandmother owned the store and her sister Francesca and friend Louise ran it for over 20 years. They've been invited to fashion shows all over the country. I came across countless articles about my grandmother's

boutique.

My mother would send Mia, Tinsley and I to Columbus

to live with my grandmother every summer, so you know

where we were every day after school and on the weekends?

That's right the boutique. Cleaning, dressing mannequins,

walking up and down the street passing out flyers. Pretty much

investing our innocent time, into this boutique. After a while,

my grandmother miss managed the store's profits, and could

only afford to keep the building up. She couldn't purchase

inventory, so she took a different approach. She would rent the

boutique out for parties and other private events. Once I went

to college, she asked if I wanted to take a stab at becoming an

entrepreneur, she actually wanted to turn the boutique over to

me and become a silent a partner. She showed me the ropes,

and all the resources; I didn't understand how she lost

business in the first place. Once my grandmother turned the

boutique over to me, I started thinking of people I knew would be great assets to my team, and just as excited about running a

boutique as I was.  Of course my sisters would work at the

store and help me run it, but I needed a few others non related

that could also make Pearl a great success.

       "I can't believe Mia wasn't there for Inventory"

Tinsley shouted as they speed the freeway rushing to

get back to the boutique.

"It's okay Tinsley, Mia does not have to be present

during every drop off," I proclaimed.

       "She does today, today Pierre's drops were made and I

don't want those nosey bitches opening boxes" Shouted

Tinsley.

       "You need to chill, besides the truck is scheduled to

arrive at 1p, it's only 1:20p. I'm sure they are still pulling boxes

off the truck we'll be there in no time.

       "You better hope so, if anything goes wrong with

Pierre's packages he's going to kill me," Tinsley decreed as she

pulled a stick of gum out of her purse.

Tinsley was a fire cracker, she was that "do anything for a man type." Her man could say jump, and best believe that bitch will do it and say, "You want me to do again." She was two years younger than me and her attitude was steaming through the roof. She fought everyone on our staff over her no good ass boyfriend Pierre Bradley, also known as Grand. He thought he was the shit. That nigga was your typical flashy but trashy type. He splurged with everything he did, but had no common sense. He felt like everybody owed him respect and because he had money the streets better abide. Dumb fucks I swear. Tinsley was my sister and I loved her, but the way he had her nose wide open was ridiculous. He kept my sister in the middle of his mess. He knew she'd do it. Making runs for him, playing the middleman to his bullshit. Tinsley had a fair complexion with sandy brown hair that ran down the center of her back. Her measurements were 36, 24, 38(< how to list measurements).

Tinsley was a very attractive female with a luscious build that men loved. Pierre and Tinsley have known each other since we were younger. His family lived across the street from our grandparents so Tinsley would spend every other weekend in his face, until he got a car. Notice I said car, no license. He took her virginity and they've been together off and on since. Tinsley has gotten into so many fights over this pathetic excuse for a man. So of course I've had my run in's over her beef. I can't say I agreed with the way Tinsley handled things, but that was my sister and I never wanted to see her hurt or in physical altercations over a no good ass man but, I love her. She never listened to anything I said when it came to Pierre. I can't stand him. He's so disrespectful and just ugly. The only thing I could say about the bastard was, he was making money from hustling, and was damn good at his operation. He had his own damn team making his runs. Pierre has been pushing weight through our boutique for the past 2 years. I just thank God we haven't been caught. The only reason he has been getting away with it was because he knew for each drop I needed at least two thousand. Our shipment came in twice a week! Pierre was well connected and only had his big

money makers coming to the boutique to pick up his product.

My grandmother would have a heart attack if she knew what

the hell was going on underneath the tables at her boutique,

but I needed the extra money to stay ahead. I wanted to prove

to my grandmother that I can handle owning the store.

Honestly Me Me Priss has only walked in here a handful of

times to see how business was going and of course we didn't

have drugs flung out in the open but, she would know

suspicious activity if she seen it. She respected my turn around

and how I handled things. She passed it along to me because

she felt I had the same fashion mind she did. My senior year of

high school, we starting promoting Pearl harder than ever. We

got our name out with the parties we through at the boutique.

My grandmother actually thought it was a great marketing tool,

plus it was near our college campus, so my school friends

thought they were walking amongst college partiers. My

grandmother knew Tinsley and I both loved fashion and what

better way to bring in money of our own than having our own

boutique to make it out of. Tinsley and I kept the name Pearl.

Tinsley hated the name and was totally against it. She's been

trying her damn best to change shit since she started working

here. I tell my mother about Tinsley's bullshit and her having

Pierre up and through the store all of the time. But my mother

advises me that Tinsley has to find her way and fall on her own.

She suggests that I should keep charging him to bring his shit

here. I actually couldn't agree more. For the last 6 months I've

been trying to devise a plan to keep Pierre in the store without

us having any involvement if he ever got caught. I figured

Pierre loved money so I'd bribe him with dollars. I convinced

him to buy the apartment up stairs and break me off 1,500 per

shipment. The address upstairs was the same address as the

boutique except we were B he was C, I figured if some shit ever

went down, I could easily persuade authorities addresses were

mixed up, and he would take full blame.  Of course the

apartment was in Tinsley's name and if some shit went down

she'd go down for it. I felt bad, but if she was dumb enough to put it in her name that was her issue. I damn sure didn't want her going to jail, but damn, I didn't want myself, or the others going to jail either. Pierre was using our inventory truck for pickups. He had it set up where deliveries would be picked up on the way to the store.

I'm sure I was seeing more money than Tinsley was from her own boyfriend. Her dumb ass was just in it for the fame. She loved him, but they had no kids and he was seen around town creeping with other bitches. We pulled up to the boutique only to find the truck still parked and Mia right at the back door giving the delivery man direction to bring in boxes.

"See, cut Mia some slack, she's here in time for inventory" I advised Tinsley as she shoved a piece of gum from her purse in her mouth.

"She better be" Tinsley stated in a stern voice.

"Where were you Mia" Tinsley questioned as she slammed my passenger door smacking on gum?

"I was at lunch two doors down, is there a problem,"
questioned Mia?

"Yea, yo ass needed to be here for inventory" Shouted
Tinsley as she bypassed Mia to get into the building.

"Shut the hell up, and help me, Mia shouted as she rolled
her eyes and continued to help the deliveryman.

Thank God Mia knew how Tinsley was, because that
was a fight ready to happen. The driver finished the UN load
and gave Pierre a call.  I went inside and pulled all boxes
loaded with Pearl's inventory inside. I left Pierre's packages in
the doorway.

"Hello Pierre, it's here," I stated to Pierre.

"Ok, I'm on the way," Pierre stated.

I went to the back of door and pulled the rest of Pierre's
boxes in and shut and locked the back door. My entire staff was
clocked in at this point. I decided to close the store for lunch
and pull the girls in for a meeting. We had a lot of things
coming up and I needed to be sure everyone was focused for

what was planned for the year. This boutique means everything to the women in my family and I was going to see to it that it ran smoothly.

"Ladies, can I see you all in the back room, everyone. Including you Tinsley," I stated as I locked the front door and flipped the out for lunch sign for our customers.

We made our way to the back room to meet in the back conference room. All of the girls took a seat, except Tinsley. Tinsley decided to stand next to me as if she was delegating my meeting. Even though we were sisters everyone knew and respected my leadership. Tinsley thought she ran shit because of relation, but she was in for a rude awakening.

"So, sales have been great, and our promotional team has been rocking out with our events. However we have just a few kinks I feel need to be worked out.  Just then, my phone rang. It was Pierre to get his boxes. I decided to take the phone call.

"Hey Mia can you take over discuss this week's floor set with the inventory that just arrived." I stated as I walked out of the door.

I met Pierre in the back as him and his boys took boxes up stairs.

"Why didn't yal take my shit upstairs? Yal was just goin' leave them here for somebody to steal," Pierre scolded!

"Listen, I don't handle that shit, now give me my money," I scolded back.

Pierre counted out my cash and placed it in my hands. I snatched the last $50 bill and rolled my eyes.

"Listen, you pretty much got me fucked up, the only thing I will do is let you use my delivery man and make drops here, you're responsible for getting them up to that apartment and they just arrived, please don't give me a hard time about them punk ass packages, or I'll cut that shit off." I proclaimed, as I counted my money.

"Yea, whatever can you send Tinsley out so I can speak with her, please your Bitchness," Pierre stated sarcastic.

"I'll go get Tinsley so you two can discuss your issues," I stated as I went to the next room.

See that nigga ran Tinsley, and for some reason he thought he ran me. He had to be corrected and every time he got out of line, I checked that shit. I walked back into the meeting room and excused Tinsley. I proceeded with my staff meeting while Tinsley handled her mess.

"Yes babe, stated Tinsley as she walked into the apartment upstairs.

"Well nothing now, shit yal left my packages in front of the door all in the open. You could have brought them up here, my packages don't need..." Pierre ranted on. In mid-sentence Tinsley dropped to her knees exposing Pierre's erection and gave him the sloppiest of sloppy head. Pierre ejaculated in Tinsley's mouth as she swallowed his cum. He became hornier. He pulled her shirt over her head and unsnapped her bra as he sat back on the couch. She unbuckled her jeans, grabbed his

penis and jumped on for a ride. She rode him while he sucked

on her nipples fingering her ass. Tinsley came all over Pierre

that afternoon; she had mastered her plan and shut his

bitching up. Tinsley knew how to shut Pierre up and that's how

she dealt with their issues, sex! I continued to conduct our

daily meeting without Tinsley that afternoon, which was best

for business.


Aside from Tinsley's immaturity, we had a pretty

dominant team. First　There was Justine I've known her since

high school. We weren't friends in High School but he both

shared and close acquaintances. She was our senior president

and I worked alongside of our senior advisors to plan school

functions. Justine was gorgeous with the most stank attitude

ever. She was all about her business. Never slacked and was

always two steps ahead. Justine had a brown complexion and

wore her hair natural. She had a very pretty natural cur and her hair reached her lower back. Justine was 38-26-40. She was curvy and carried it well. Justine attended Ohio State and graduated with a degree in finance. Then there was Isaac, Mia's friend who was our gay fashionista. Oh my God he could dress his ass off. His people were from New York and he moved here to Columbus after getting in so much trouble. He moved here his sophomore year and graduated from Reynoldsburg High School. He decided to stay here and fully commit to Pearl. (Isaac attends a fashion school in Columbus Ohio) I love him so much. He has all the connections in New York, and actually our link to our models, photo shoots and inventory. He knows everything about the latest fashion trends and honestly, more than likely the next to blow. Isaac was very clean cut. Though he was gay and took pride in that, he wasn't the flamboyant type. He dressed very casual, kept a crisp low fade and no facial hair, which was a bit odd.  Everything about Fashion, described Isaac's personality opposed to his wardrobe. Finally there was Tinsley's hood Rat friend Yvette who needed a job.  She barely came to work and got paid minimum wage due to her lack of

experience. Yvette stayed on her phone and was a fill in when I

needed an extra sales associate. Tinsley and Yvette were

running buddies and both messed with dope boys. Yvette was

a yellow little thing with a short bob cut. Measurements were

32-24-34. She was very petite. Tinsley and Yvette loved putting

things in their names for the men in their bedrooms. I never

understood the logic, but if it works for them, I guess it works

for me. At least twice a year, I would put together a trip for my

staff to head to New York during fashion week.  All of the

money I was getting under the table financed our trips. Our

business was doing all right, but not enough to finance 6

people in and out of town. I was always playing for Pearl,

however, Tinsley would always try and bring Pierre and

Yvette's brother Yasir along. Of course I would tell her ass, they

had to find their own transportation and hotel, because we

would be there for business. For the life of me I didn't

understand how someone could be so wrapped up in a man

they neglected business and progression to please the likes of another.

"Well Guy's Today, we're going to go ahead and change our store front so if I can have Yvette and Mia work on Mannequins, Isaac you can do cash wrap and I'll hang inventory," I concluded as Tinsley walked back in as if she wasn't gone the whole meeting.

"What I miss," Tinsley asked as everyone started to exit the room?

"I just went over daily tasks, nothing major, I stated as I walked toward the door.

"Yea, you're always leaving me out of shit," Shouted Tinsley!

"What, shut the hell up you knew where we were, he have daily meetings everyday same time, you just feel some type of way because you were sucking dick on the job," I proclaimed as I walked out of the room.

I could here everyone chuckle as they walked back on the sales floor.

Tinsley was always trying to flip shit to make it look like she was the victim.

Money was the objective at the end of the day. I did dirt too, but I wasn't messy with my shit. Nobody knew how I moved or any man I had been with. I kept my private life very separate.

I closed the store at 8 o'clock that night, and sent everybody home early. I finished cleaning. I had my own shit going on and needed a moment to clear my head.  I had developed a relationship with an attorney by the name of Anthony Reginald Cox a few months ago. I meet him at the pub right across the street. He had his own law firm and he was single and handsome. What more could a woman ask for.  He typically stopped by at 9 o'clock pm because we knew I would still be closing up. That night specifically, he came by a little early.  He was the type that thought he could buy love. So I knew I could milk him out of something. At first money was the

motive but the more we spent time together the more

interested I became.  I heard a knock on the front door and saw

him standing outside with a bottle of Champaign. I opened the

door and let him in. I walked him to the back office and closed

the door.

"Well, well, well. What brings you here this evening," I

asked playfully as I peeped my pencil skirt hug my ass through

the mirror across the room.

"Well first off this, is what brings me here," Anthony

stated as he grabbed my ass.

I turned around, sat on the table and pulled him in for a

kiss.  We kissed as both of us undressed each other. Pulling my

breasts out of my shirt I unbuckled his pants to expose his

manhood. He handed me a condom and I slid it on. I hopped on

top and rode him like a dirt bike. I knew he was guaranteed to

leave some money on the table the way I was riding him. I hula

hooped around and started riding him from the back. I grabbed the back of his legs and thrashed his man hood into my vagina.

His legs buckled and I could see him getting weak. I could feel

his legs trembling. I lowered him into the swivel chair next to

the table. I backed up on him as he held on for the ride. He sat

his ass cheeks on the leather chair and sat back as I massaged

his balls while I ride him. I gave him his ultimate dream come

true. I left his mind blown while I gave him a special incentive

for being my playboy. See a playboy is that man who likes to

spend, wine and dine women while getting sexual attention, no

strings attached. The basic bitch might refer to him as a trick,

freak or her bitch. Even though these men acted like hounding

animals, there was no need to treat them as such. I wanted this

situation to last as long as possible. Why not be with someone

I'm physically attracted to, only! There was no class about

being a hoe, but if you're going to do it, it has to be discreet. I

didn't put a price on my box, but if any man wanted this love he

had to pay. This game between Anthony and I was competition,

He would only pay if I made him nut, and I did that just about every time. He licked up his mess and left 2500 on the table. I walked Anthony out of the back door. I opened the door and caught Pierre smoking on the back step. He snickered and greeted Anthony as Anthony walked past toward the side of the building.

"Bye Babe," I shouted!

I wanted Pierre to think that was my man and there was no need to think any further into it.

Anthony didn't even bother to say it back. I was so addicted to money; revenue was being produced from every aspect of my life.

I left Pearl at midnight and headed home ready to count these funds. I had a lot running through my mind and needed rest. I arrived at my condo and noticed Mia standing in front of my door. She still lived at home with our parents but had a key to her boyfriend's place here. My sisters knew they could come to my place any time they needed. They each had a key but apparently Mia forgot hers.

"Mia, are you okay," I whispered?

She lifted her head and I could see her eyes all swollen from crying. I unlocked my door, grabbed Mia's arm and walked in. She stared at me as tears fell from her face.

"What's the matter," I asked as I grabbed her head into my chest.

"Wayne wants to get married, he wants to have kids, he wants us to start a family and we're only 22 and 23. I'm not ready for that," Mia screamed.

"Well that doesn't mean you have to be sad lil sis. If you're not ready Wayne will understand, he's a good guy," I advised.

"Exactly, and now I'm pregnant right. Birth Control and condoms still couldn't prevent that right. Such a great guy my ass. How did I get pregnant," Mia proclaimed as she wiped her face.

I was speechless. If Mia said she took her pills and used condoms, I believed her. She was very conservative and not fast at all. Having a boyfriend was a stretch for her.

"Well maybe you skipped a day," I stated.

"Maybe the condom broke," I added.

"You know what, I thought about that, but no! I always remembered taking my pills and I bought us condoms every two weeks. He has been pressuring me to have kids for the last few weeks. I'm not keeping it," Mia shouted hysterically.

"Mia, you've got to calm down," I stated as I grabbed Mia's shoulders to face her square in the eye.

"You have to think about this with your brain, you knew what you were doing, you laid down with him unprotected. These are the consequences," I declared.

"Dionne, did you hear me, I never had sex with him without a condom. Wayne knew the routine, there was a condom in place before each session no doubt," Mia proclaimed!

"Even your drunk days," I questioned her right back

"NO! Not even on a drunken day. Besides, his ass always gets drunk and passes out until the morning,"

"Oh, wow! He set you up," I stated!

"What, you think this nigga planned this," Mia questioned as her brain wondered?

I instantly grew emotional to the thought of Mia being extra careful.  This ass hole really trapped my sister. I grabbed the absolute bottle from the fridge and poured me up a shot. Mia insisted I pour her up a few shots as well. We sat in my living room talking and discussing future plans for the store. Mia was very excited and aspired to be the face of pearl so she could kick off her career in modeling.  She had already done parties for our local entertainment and cameos in a few videos. She absolutely was disgusted with the thought of being pregnant. She knew that her perfect figure would be destroyed once she had the baby.

The next morning I arrived at the store to open. I walked to the front door and noticed a note from Anthony. He had let me know he stopped by and wanted to see me, the letter said that he wanted a piece of me on the store floor. I unlocked the front door and noticed Isaac sitting underneath the awning outside the front of the store with his head in his lap. I opened the door, peaked out and called his name.

"Ike, what the hell, you ok," I yelled?

He raised his right hand and gave me thumbs up.

"I'm good bitch," he yelled as I walked back inside.

I could have only imagined what he did the night before.

However, he did make it to work on time. I have to love him for that. See, Ike was my most honest and loyal employee. He told me 100 percent truth to whatever he was feeling, and his ideas of fashion. His opinions mean, a lot of chatting with clients, clients mean word of mouth and word of mouth means money! I'd say Ike refers 70 percent of my clientele. I cut his ass in heavy around back. Anytime Pierre pays me, I pay myself and then I pay Ike.  On top of the money he was making at the store. I guess you can say we were intimate friends whenever we were in the mood as well. If Ike ever wanted to find out what the womankind was like, I'd tell him, or show him whichever came first. He's never penetrated my box, but I would let him slide his fingers in between to get a feel for womanhood.

My sexual pride was all about my, no man left behind rule.  I couldn't help myself; Isaac was an attractive gay man. I've never taken it further than that though. Hell it was a great experience for me.

Sales were boosting top of spring. We had a few events coming up and ready to launch our new jean line called Anchor Jeans. The cut of the jean was for our curvy customers. Majority of our clientele had ass, so we had to support the ass epidemic.  We all decided to do a club night event.  We were planning on staying open until 2 am to get club goers in the area ready to go out.  We would have local make-up artist and hairstylist come out to the boutique for packaged services. We offered select services to customers spending over three hundred dollars with Pearl.

Those customers would receive a complementary hairstyle and makeup service. I was so excited for Pearl's first Club Night event. It would be the ultimate shopping experience. In addition to our Club night event, Pearl would be featured in a huge fashion show in a few weeks. Some of the models would be wearing a few of our pieces and we were really excited about our spring line.

I banged on the restroom door to see if Isaac was ok. He opened the door reeking of mouthwash.

"Well I'm glad you smell refreshed," I stated as I squinted my eyes to check his face.

"Yea I really didn't drink that much," Isaac stated as he straightened his chin hair.

"Yeah, that's what they all say," I responded as I cut open a box shipped in.

"I can't believe this is happening for us, we've been waiting for this fashion show to kick off for months," Ike shouted as he yanked the inventory out of the boxes.

"Okay well calm down before you rip something, and grab those boxes behind you, and get to cutting. Sweet cheeks,"

"The fashion show is going to be huge, but we have to make it through our club night event first," I corrected.

He hated when I got bossy with him. Hell, everybody needed to know I don't play when it comes to my boutique. A corporation didn't run us. This was a mom and popshop, so we were all family. I was the head of the team. Without my authorities, this place would go up in shambles. They respected that, and that's all I asked.

The rest of today's staff wouldn't be in until 11"0clock am. Mia went to school on Friday's so she didn't come in at all. Ike was the only one to come in early with me on Friday's. He treated this place just like me. Everything he involved his self in was about fashion. He was my trendsetter and I trusted his opinion more than my own sister's.

"So, Dionne I'm going to a private party tonight at the Hyatt, do you want to come with," questioned Isaac as he hung our new inventory in the back.

"Private party, who's in town," I questioned.

A private party only meant that there was someone big here. Isaac always had the connections, He thought of me first when he got invites to exclusive events. I worked so damn much I forgot that I even had a social life. I accepted Isaac's invitation to the party and immediately started to think of what I would wear. We had a good productive day in the boutique. I closed business as normal that day. I lived a block away from the boutique so Isaac and I went to my place to get dressed after work.

We closed up the boutique as normal and headed to my condo.

"Hey Dionne, do you think I'm crossing boundaries if I invite my friend to our club night event," Isaac asked?

I was a little uncertain why he felt he was crossing boundaries. "Well you know I don't care who you bring, you're a good judge of character, I know it wouldn't be any body that would threaten us or our business. Why would you be crossing boundaries," I questioned.

"Tinsley did tell you about the incident at the boutique the other night when you were in Chicago visiting your parents, right," Isaac asked.

"Uhmm No!, she didn't tell me anything. What incident, I asked in complete confusion.

"Oh damn, I would have been told you had I known you didn't know anything." Isaac informed as I stared at him while making my way up the street.

"Giiiiirrrrrl, your sister is fucking with a down low brotha," He quickly blurted out.

I stopped in my tracks, as I tried to soak in the information Isaac just gave me.

"Who, Mia or Tinsley," I questioned realizing I have two sisters with bitch niggas.

"Tinsley's man, Honey," Stated Isaac!

"What, Pierre's on the low, how did this come about, how did you find out," I questioned.

I was trying to make sense of this hood nigga being someone's bitch. I mean Pierre has his ways, but I couldn't imagine him of all people. I mean he has bitches all over this city. He was always at the strip clubs and indulging in other women. Isaac wouldn't come with half ass information, if he knew something more than likely it was accurate.

"So, what happened at the store while I was gone," I questioned as Isaac took a deep breath.

"Well I was going to get a few drinks with friends after work. They came in right before we closed and waited for me to finish filing paperwork in the back. Supposedly my friend

Ryan saw Pierre talking to Tinsley at the cash register and yelled his nickname. I guess Pierre turned and looked at him and smacked his lips, and said, "you don't know me homie,"

"Ryan said he was pissed, he said he didn't blurt out anything disrespectful and they were locked up together not even a year prior. He said he was confused as to why Pierre was acting like that. Ryan said he got up and started walking toward him laughing like, Grand it's me Ryan, remember we were locked up in Noble together," Isaac shared.

As Isaac told the story, I could only imagine the thoughts going through Tinsley's mind. She never expressed to me what happened at the store that day. She knew how I felt about Pierre's shifty ass. I continued to listen to Isaac finish telling me about the incident that day.  I had it  made up in my mind that Tinsley was going to get an ear full about this.

"Ryan said as he got closer to Pierre he grabbed him and threw him damn near across the room. Ryan said he was pissed but didn't want to disrespect the store. He said he wanted to expose him instead. He said he got up chuckled and said oh you may as well kiss your reputation goodbye. I walked out of the back room and I saw Mia checking on Ryan outside," Isaac explained as we entered my condo elevators.

"I just don't understand why Pierre would put his hands on him, knowing that he has dirt on him," I questioned confused as to why Pierre think he is so damn untouchable.

"Because he's a dumb ass, the secret's out now! You need to have a sit down with your sister and find out where her head is. Ryan already discussed putting a plan in motion to blast his ass," Isaac quickly replied back.

He was right I needed to talk to Tinsley, but I was in the middle of a good time, so I disregarded their issue for the rest of the evening.

Isaac and I made our way to my condo. I walked in and flipped on the media player. Beyoncé Pandora poured through the speakers. Destiny's Child- Jumpin' had me rockin. I was in full party mode, but I was on a mission to network.

I immediately got into party mode. Even though this wasn't going to be a kick it party for me, my confidence needed to be on that level. Things were moving in a steady pace for the boutique and I wanted to keep it that way. My mind was always focused on my money, even when I joined social gatherings. I pulled out a form fitting emerald green dress. It was 100% polyester with the spandex lining so you know it was fitting. It had a lower back scoop and it came a few inches below my knee. I had my favorite designer Wieland Jeffery send me a sample when he featured a similar one in his fashion show. That was the glory about attending social gatherings. Whenever you go to any social gatherings you know other partygoers will be there dressed in their hottest fashion. I was hoping I'd come across one person who has a small retail business as well. I may come across someone who knows someone who does. Word of mouth is your biggest tool, if you talk about the things that interest you, your success will follow. I damn sure was a motor mouth when it came to Pearl. I thrived on fashion, and new trends were always my topics of

discussion.  These small social gatherings were so important to

my business. They've bought me a lot of clientele. I get stuff

sent in all the time. If we have anything going on, I try to

feature another designer's piece at our events. Just to show

support to the other entrepreneurs. Isaac and I made our way

to the party that night. We had an amazing time and meet a lot

of designers and new stylist in the area who were interested in

shopping with us.

# ALTAMATUMS

Mia made it home to her boyfriend Wayne after school that night. Whenever Mia was in Columbus she shared a little apartment on the outer skirts of Columbus with Wayne, however her primary address was in Chicago with our parents. Mia had been completely stressed out the last few weeks. She found out she was pregnant and 100 percent sure that her boyfriend somehow trapped her into it. Mia had stayed with me for a few nights after she found out. She had advised me that she didn't feel like dealing with Wayne and his bullshit just yet. Mia decided to go home that night after school. She had been telling him that I had her in the store late nights and she just wanted to crash with me. Mia walked into her apartment expecting the night to be filled with emotions arguments and an excuse to leave.

"Hey babe," Wayne called out as Mia entered the front door.

"Hey," Mia replied as she sat her bags down in front of the front door.

She had walked into a brand new living room. Mia had been saying she wanted to re do their living room together and apparently the few days Mia was staying with me, Wayne took it upon his self and surprised her with a new sectional, a brand new TV and he had painted the walls a new color. Wayne had the whole living room fully decorated and ready for his woman to live in it. He assumed she would love the surprise and melt in his arms when she discovered it. Me personally loved the idea. I would love to come to a brand new living area, especially if I had the intentions on changing it one day soon. Mia grew even more upset. She walked upstairs for a shower to relax her mind before she flipped out on Wayne for his constant controlling. Mia was over Wayne's managing attitude and the way he wanted to live life. First planning a pregnancy that she didn't want, then re decorating the living room she wanted to decorate herself.  Wayne could sense the hostility he had been getting from Mia and the way she stormed in must've been the last straw. Wayne stormed through the door and opened the shower door while Mia showered.

"What the hell is wrong with you," shouted Wayne!

"Wayne its cold please shut the door," Mia instructed as she tried to reach for the door.

Wayne pulled the door open even wider so Mia couldn't reach.

"No, get out and talk to me or you'll never take a shower in this house again," Wayne demanded.

"Are you threatening me," Mia questioned.

"You're the one who needs to be explaining, and since you're redecorating I know you found the pregnancy test," Mia shouted as she wrapped herself with a towel.

"Yea you're right, I did find the pregnancy test. That's why I didn't pressure you to come here. I know you're

45

pregnant and you wouldn't be doing anything with anyone else," Wayne confirmed as he chuckled.

"What, what the hell type of mentality is that. You should be fucking worried. I'm pregnant by you. We've never discussed kids, and you're just all nonchalant like it doesn't matter," Mia scolded.

"It shouldn't matter. You got a man that wants to marry you, what's the hold up. I want you to have my kids Mia, that's why I did it. I want you all to myself. I want you to be mine forever. Our relationship has been through enough. Let's just make it happen," Wayne explained.

In Wayne's mind this was ok. Where he came from, men on a daily, dogged females. He felt that because he wanted marriage and kids that should be sufficient enough. He believed he was a good man and Mia should submit to his desires.

"Wayne do you even know what I want," Mia questioned as she paced back and forth in front of him.

"What about what the hell Mia wants Wayne," Mia shouted.

"Babe, you're trippin' if you don't want the baby just get an abortion, and that's pretty much all I have to say about it. You're being stupid, you want me to apologize for loving you and wanting a family with the woman I love. I don't understand you broad's man. I'm out," Wayne shouted as he reached for a pair of tennis shoes out of the closet.

"You know what this is some bull shit, you lay down your demands and then you leave. I'm the one standing here pregnant because you trapped me, then you're upset because this wasn't something I wanted, and you tell me to just get an abortion. You can't be fucking serious right now," Mia yelled as she stood over top of Wayne as he tied his shoes.

"We need to discuss this, we need to find a resolution tonight, this is insane," Mia declared as she reached for her robe.

"Wayne Listen," She sat down next to Wayne and grabbed his hand.

In an instant Wayne felt Mia's sincerity. He knew that she was bothered and he had to fix it.

"It's been me and you babe for quite some time now. We've done everything together. We've always had the same interest and ideas; we never had problems about other people in our relationship, so why wouldn't you trust me with a decision such as a baby," Mia insisted as she looked him square in the face.

"Wayne it's like you made the decision for me. You didn't give me an opportunity to decide on what I wanted to do. Had I known you were that adamant about having kids, I may have compromised with you," Mia advised.

"Well now you know, the decision has been made. You're carrying my baby, and now we can work towards getting married," Wayne instructed as Mia rolled her eyes and became uncomfortable all over again. It was clear Wayne was already set in his own ways and Mia could not make him understand that his dominant personality was destroying his relationship. Mia stopped talking altogether about Wayne's controlling ways.  She figured she was pregnant, which may not be the worst thing in the world, but she believed in things happening for specific reasons. Mia accepted her pregnancy that day. She did however decide that she would not accept Wayne's controlling ass.  She knew she had a lot to think about. She decided to go home to Chicago for the rest of the weekend so she could clear her mind.

"I can't believe this idiot thinks he's a man because he wants kids and shit," Mia said aloud to herself as she drove the expressway toward Chicago to her father's house.

"The last thing I need is a controlling ass man trying to dictate my life," Mia declared.

Mia pulled up to her father's house and noticed Tinsley's car parked in the driveway.

"Whhhhaaaaaat, this bitch crawled from up under that niggas ass," Mia said in the car to herself as she examined the house and noticed the living room lights on.

Mia walked in the house and noticed Eileen and Tinsley sitting in the front living room talking on the couch. Mia noticed Tinsley's eyes watery and puffy. She knew she had been crying, and couldn't help but to assume it was about Pierre.

"Hey Ladies, what's going on," Mia questioned as she walked in and noticed the conversation mute when she entered the room.

"Well Hello Mia, nothing much, Tinsley and I are just sitting here having girl talk," Eileen quickly responded.

"Oh, ok. Well what's wrong with you Tins," Mia questioned Tinsley unsatisfied with Eileen's quick response.

"Pierre broke up with me," Tinsley replied.

"Oh, wow, well you guys will work it out, Mia responded.

Mia instantly regretted asking Tinsley what was wrong. She had a few opinions about their situation, but decided this may not have been a good time to bring it up. Mia followed the grand staircase up to her room. She entered her room and sat her things down. As soon as Mia got comfortable she heard a knock at the door.

"Come in," she yelled toward the door.

She noticed Tinsley's face appear from behind the door.

"Hey, what's wrong with you," Mia questioned as Tinsley entered.

Mia didn't expect Tinsley's visit to be about Pierre. Tinsley knew no one in the house accepted Pierre, nor did they have anything nice to say about him.

"Mia, what's wrong with me," Tinsley questioned as she lay across Mia's bed.

"What do you mean, I personally feel you have a little growing up to do, but other than that nothing is wrong with you," Mia responded.

"How come I'm not a good judge of character," Tinsley asked?

"I mean, I should be able to pick a cheater right out of any line up," Tinsley proclaimed.

"A cheater no, you wouldn't be able to tell if someone's a cheater just by simply looking at them. You and Pierre have been through a lot, but it seems to me you have a lot more to worry about than just cheating," Mia insisted.

"Well cheating is the only thing we've really argued about," Tinsley corrected.

"I heard him on the phone with a girl when I walked into the apartment today. Then he hangs up all fast, and while I'm questioning him, she starts calling his phone back to back. He didn't answer the phone the whole time I stood there, Tinsley explained.

"Yea, but aside from this argument did you ask him about Ryan, Mia asked in confusion.

The accusations of a gay man holding information on a straight more was far more important than him being on the phone with some chick.

"There was nothing to ask, Ryan walked up on him and Pierre got mad. Pierre doesn't like anyone in his space," Tinsley responded.

"Ok, no you need to ask that man what the hell was Ryan talking about. Ryan seems to have dirt on him. You don't think that was the reason behind Pierre acting like that, that day, Mia counseled.

"I mean we didn't talk about it, I didn't want to bring it up because he seemed to be really upset about it after we left. He even called his boy's to stomp out Isaac and Ryan after the party we're having at the boutique," Tinsley expressed.

"Listen Tinsley, I know I don't get in your business and you're an adult, but Pierre just walks all over you. Fuck these bitches calling his phone, that's the least of your worries. You need to pay attention. Ryan has dirt on him, and when a gay man has dirt it's typically really dirty. Use your brain. Think of a plan to leave Pierre before you end up worse off.  Stop trying to be that man's wife without being that man's wife. I mean really. He's never even bought you a ring. You have to stop giving so much only to get nothing in the end. You deserve better and you know it," Mia lectured as Tinsley buried her face and started to sob.

"It's like everybody feels like they need to judge me, because my life isn't as great as yours or Dionne's, you and Dionne seem to have it all figured out right. You guys just look down on me because I was the troublemaker right, like people can't change," Tinsley yelled through her sobbing tears.

"When are you going to be satisfied with Tinsley? When are you going to feel like that nigga needs you rather than you needing him? When the hell are you going to get what you want? When the hell are you going to listen to your sisters, you don't get the replies you were hoping for and you get upset with us. You either want better or you don't. Go check his ass, not us," Mia proclaimed as Tinsley wiped her face.

Even when Mia voiced her opinions, it was always from a loving place. Even though we didn't talk about our personal lives on a daily we still were very aware of each other's circumstance. We all had each other's back and would do anything for each other.

"Well, Mia you got you something nice with a loving and caring man. So I do listen to you. Everyone knows Wayne loves and adores you. I want to have that effect on Pierre," Tinsley stated.

"Well shit on him, deal with his ass on your time, and focus on nobody but Tinsley, and he'll be crawling back before you know it, Mia suggested.

"I never thought I would see the day, my baby sister would be giving me relationship advice," Tinsley stated as she reached for Mia's phone ringing in front of her. Tinsley noticed someone named Lamont calling Mia's phone. She handed Mia's phone straight to her and decided to listen in.

"Hey you, what are you doing," Mia said in her most sexy voice Tinsley ever heard.

"Yea that's coo, we can link up. Do you want me to meet you there," Mia questioned as she opened the closet to find something to wear.

"Ok that's fine, I'll call you as soon as I get dressed, Mia stated as she hung up with her phone call. She turned around toward Tinsley and noticed her staring at her.

"So who was that, Tinsley questioned following Mia around her room with her eyes.

"A friend," Mia responded.

"A friend! Does Wayne know about this friend," Tinsley asked.

"No he doesn't, I'm enjoying some time with an old friend right now. And Wayne doesn't need to know anything about it," Mia clarified as she grabbed Tinsley's arm to lead her out of her room.

"See you have a good man, and you want to cheat on him, I can't get my man to stay faithful, Tinsley explained.

Tinsley it's more complicated than you think, it's just a friendly meet up with an old friend, Mia argued.

"Yea ok, I'll leave and let you get ready for your lil date but, you think about the mess your dear old sister is in before you decide to cheat, and that's all I'm going to say," Tinsley shouted as she slammed the door behind her.

Mia just wanted a little free time. No one knew Mia was even pregnant except me. No one even knew the extent of Mia's relationship except me.  It had become way more complicated since the pregnancy. Mia was totally oblivious to who Wayne had become. Wayne had completely changed. He had become much more demanding and this was a side Mia hadn't encountered. Mia decided to meet her longtime friend Lamont at the Navy Pier. Mia and Lamont decided to grab something to eat and catch up. Mia and Lamont decided to spend the night together. Lamont prepared a hotel room for them that night. Mia and Lamont arrived in a hotel room in down town Chicago. Lamont noticed Mia's tall and slender physique waiting to be touched. Mia was 5'10 brown skinned and dark brown hair shoulder length. Lamont loved everything about Mia when they were younger and now he was in love with what she became. Lamont was 6 foot even, so Mia fit perfectly in his arms.

"So you live in Columbus now," Lamont asked as he pulled Mia's jacket off.

"Not permanently, but I am there 80 percent of the time working in our family boutique," Mia replied.

"Oh yea, that's right, you ladies still have your boutique," Lamont questioned in complete astonishment that the boutique was still open.

"Hell yea we still open. We have a few things coming up, you should come down and check it out," Mia suggested as she reached in her purse and handed Lamont a flyer inviting him to the up and coming Club Night event that Pearl would be hosting. Mia reached down to pick up the drink menu up from the table in the hotel room.

"Good, Good! Would you like a drink," Lamont offered.

Lamont has always been a gentleman. He was so sweet and gentle. Never really heard of him being an asshole. He came from a great family, and he was into his self. No kids, just an all-around ladies' man. I could've seen Mia with him when they were younger, but for whatever reason it didn't work out.

"Actually I shouldn't drink tonight, I've been on the road all day, and it'll just make me sleepy," Mia responded, realizing she was 6 weeks pregnant.

"Oh, ok suit yourself, I'll pour me some cognac, since you're not drinking," Lamont declared as he poured his self a double shot of cognac.

Even though Mia was carrying Wayne's baby, she could only think about his controlling ways.  She couldn't help but think about how she wanted to escape her current situation for a little breathing room. The only thing on Mia's mind that night was relaxation.

Lamont took his shot to the head and started disrobing out of his clothes. He unbuttoned his shirt and pulled off his undershirt exposing his huge triceps and biceps and six pack abs. Mia's personal thoughts had become blank after she witnessed a man made to perfection.

"You ok," Lamont asked, as he caught Mia's mouth wide open and mind in another time zone.

"Yes I'm fine, I mean your fine, I mean…." Lamont let off a loud chuckle as Mia tried to cover up her thoughts.

"So what's up with you and your boyfriend," Lamont asked as Mia scrambled for words, realizing that this man must think I'm a slut. He knows I have a boyfriend, and clearly things are heating up.

"Well we're not seeing eye to eye right now. Actually he broke up with me," Mia fabricated, not wanting to tell too much of her business to her old friend.

"Anyone that brakes up with you is a clown, he doesn't deserve you. If you were my woman, you'd be right here in my arms tonight," Lamont stated as he pulled Mia in closer to him.

Lamont decided to go in for the kill, kissing Mia into a trance. Everything that Mia had on her mind had disappeared. All of the feelings and emotions she once had for Lamont had somehow come back all in an instant. Mia's hormones took over her mind that night.

Mia climbed on top of Lamont to adjust her body over top of him.  He slowly undressed Mia, embracing the center of her back. He licked her from her neck down the center of her back reaching the crack of her ass. Lamont flipped Mia over while reaching for a condom. Mia grabbed for his manhood and began to stroke him. She grabbed the condom and secured it for a ride.

Lamont was very gentle with Mia and was surprised she was taking control. Mia and Lamont had never had sex together, Lamont wanted to make sure their first time very special.

Lamont guided his manhood into Mia's honey pot. As she moaned her tight lips griped his huge cock. Repeatedly deep stroking, Mia's moans became louder and louder as Lamont's stroke made her climax before she could say his name. Mia completely zoned out. Neglecting the entire fact that she was carrying Wayne's baby inside of her. Lamont embraced Mia's ass that night. He pulled out and massaged her back while inserting his fingers in her inner joy. Mia's juice overflowed all over the hotel sheets. Lamont enjoyed every inch of Mia's body in his presence that night. He made her laugh, held chatted about old times and kissed the entire night away.

"Maim, I have you on the meter," The Chicago Cab driver reminded Mia as she searched for her keys.

Mia decided to leave Lamont a note and catch a cab home the next morning. Between the long stroking and the baby Mia was carrying, morning sickness set in as soon as the sunset.  Mia snatched her dress off of the hook in the hotel room and slid on her shoes. The nausea was getting worse and she could feel herself about to be sick. She wrote Lamont a small note telling Lamont that there was a family emergency and that she had to be back home. She told Lamont that he could call her once he woke up. She ran to the lobby restroom as fast as she could. Mia arrived just in time as everything inside of her, spilled out into the toilet of the women restroom.

"Whew thank God! I knew this was about to happen," Mia stated as she wiped vomit from her mouth. Mia reached for the travel size mouthwash in her purse and gargled. Mia spit out the mouthwash followed by more vomit. She couldn't control her sickness. She was sweating and she still didn't feel well. Mia gargled again, this time immediately grabbing a hand full of cold water from the sink to wash down whatever was trying to come up.

"Oh Dear God this is going to be a long pregnancy," Mia said to herself as she grabbed her purse from the sink counter. Mia ran downstairs to meet the cab that she reserved parked out front.

"Sir, just a second I'm looking for my keys," Mia shouted to the cabby and she shook her purse for rattling keys. She pulled her keys out of the side pocket of her purse and jumped in the cab.

Mia gave the cab driver her address and headed home. Mia instantly thought about the night she spent with Lamont. For one night her mind was free of all the bullshit and drama that clouded her life the day before. At that very moment she could care less what the hell Wayne was up to.

"Hey Mia, I've been calling you since last night, look baby I know you're upset but we need to talk, be at my place tonight. I have a surprise for you," Wayne decided to leave Mia a voicemail. After several unanswered phone calls Wayne began to worry about his pregnant girlfriend. Wayne decided to head to the boutique to see if Mia had gotten to work.

"Hey Justine what's up, Mia make in to work yet," Wayne asked Justine as he walked into the boutique.

"Mia actually called in this morning she won't be here until tonight. She works tonight, we have a floor set overnight," Justine confirmed, as Wayne grew even more enraged.

"Is everything ok," Justine asked as she came from around the cash wrap.

"I've been looking for Mia all night. She won't answer I just don't understand. We got into a huge fight and I haven't heard from her since," Wayne explained fishing for information on where Mia was.

"Well last night she was in Chicago at home. She said she was driving down this afternoon in time for work tonight," Justine confirmed as Wayne looked outside the door.

"She told you this," Wayne questioned enthusiastically.

"Yea when she called in this morning," Justine replied.

"You two will be fine, I'm sure she just needed a little time to clear her mind," Justine encouraged.

"You know Mia hates confrontation, Justine advised as she went back to work leaving Wayne in the middle of the sales floor.

"Yea you're right, well when she gets in tell her I've been looking for her," Wayne shouted as he walked toward the front door to leave.

"I can't believe this, Mia hasn't answered any of my calls. She's running around pregnant with my child and actually thinks I won't come looking for her. She either comes home tonight or stays away forever.

# TALK OF THE CITY

"I can't wait until our club night event. Two designers from Chicago emailed me this morning, they want to send me two pieces to feature that night," I explained to the girls as we prepared for the day.

Nobody seemed to be excited that we were having a club night event, except me. When we have events we go all out.  I have a hairstylist and a makeup artist dedicating their time to us for the night and no one is excited.

"Dionne, Mia called this morning she said she wouldn't be in until tonight," Also one of the girls you asked to model for the club night event wanted to know if she could bring three additional girls to work the event, also shipment will be late this week." Justine read from her paper. She jotted down the messages she had received before I got to work.

"Aside from all the other bullshit I was dealing with, shipment will be late," I shouted as I stormed back to my office.

I didn't feel like dealing with anyone's drama. I just wanted to focus on the event and move forward from there.

Just as I sat down in my chair I heard a knock at my office door.

"Come in I yelled," Justine appeared from behind the door.

"Dionne I just want to let you know, I have your back. We all do, everything is taken care of for the event the DJ, food, hairstylist, makeup artist, everything. We are going to get shipment a few hours late but nothing we can't handle. We've all committed to working over if need be for the shipment to be placed at the store.

Justine turned to walk out of my office door.

"Justine, I know I don't tell you much, but thank you. You are very professional and you always handle business the correct way." I said to Justine as she smiled and walked out of my office.

I know Justine holds her opinions to herself a lot of the time, but everything isn't all peaches and cream in the real world, but for what she does, I really appreciate her.

I logged on Facebook to update my status about this week's event; verify if guest were coming because I had been hearing everyone has been super excited about it. I scrolled down my time line only to see Pierre's rant about gay men. I mean He bashed damn near every gay man locally known in this city.

"Why the fuck is he being a jerk," I said aloud as I scrolled through recent posts.

I know I would hear about it. Everyone knew that Pierre was my sister's boyfriend, and everyone in the streets of Columbus knew Pierre.

I walked out of my office and could hear Justine on her phone in the meeting room. I could always count on her to handle things and get things done. That night we closed the boutique and immediately got started on our new floor set for this Saturday. Mia knocked on the front door for someone to open the door.

"Well hello Ms. M.I.A," I stated as we chuckled together.

"Hey, how was business today," Mia questioned as she put her bags down.

"Business was good today, your man stopped by looking for you earlier, although I wasn't here, but Justine said he was pissed," I explained to Mia as she grabbed my arm and led me to my office.

"Dionne, I did some fucked up shit, but I don't feel bad about it," Mia explained.

"Oh shit, what'd you do," I questioned.

"I had sex with an ex-boyfriend from back home," Just then Justine barged in my office to give me the telephone.

"Oh Mia, did Dionne tell you that Wayne stopped by earlier," Justine stopped and faced Mia to wait for her response.

"Yea, she told me actually that's what we were just discussing. So what did he say," Mia questioned.

"He said he had been looking for you all day, and wondered if you were here. I told him you were driving back from Chicago this morning, Justine explained.

"He seemed really upset Mia, maybe you should call and talk to him. He was really concerned, if you guys are together, he has a right to know what's going on with you," Justine suggested as Mia looked at Justine.

"Thanks Justine," Mia stated as she turned back toward me to tell me about Chicago.

Justine walked out of my office. There was a lot of drama going on outside of the boutique, but for some reason everyone was bringing his or her bullshit here.  I was drama free and nigga free and that seemed to work best for me.

"Dionne, was I wrong for that," Mia questioned as she paced the floor.

"Yes honey, that was very wrong technically you guys are still together, so you cheated on him, but why did you cheat. Was it because he got you pregnant against your will, I questioned.

"I mean yea, it is. I mean he is acting crazy Dionne; he wants to control my every move. He wants to dictate what I do and when I do it, he doesn't give a damn that I don't want a baby," Mia explained as she tried to make sense of having sex with another man while carrying her boyfriend's baby.

"I know baby sis, but you can't have sex with other men while pregnant just because you're mad at your boyfriend. Different stoke for different folk, and you don't need to be getting stroked," I said out loud laughing.

"Whhhhew, I laughed hysterically out loud at my own joke.

"Mia, I wouldn't tell him. You clearly needed a getaway for a night and you got one. You just can't let it happen again. Not while you're pregnant at least," I proclaimed.

Mia always kept her love life between her and Wayne, but for some reason, she couldn't make sense of what Wayne was doing to her life. Why does he think he can dictate her having a baby? I felt so bad for my baby sisters. They were both having relationship troubles meanwhile I was worried about making this money.

Mia and I walked back to the sales floor to finish with the floor set.  They knew at work it was hard getting any relationship advice from me. I promised her dinner after we left the boutique to finish our discussion about Wayne, I'm glad I knew what was going on with her. My girls would be at work on edge, snapping at everybody, I'm just glad she told me.

"Dionne did you see Pierre in the back when you came out of your office," Tinsley asked walking toward the back of the boutique.

"No, I didn't see him back there," I responded.

Tinsley walked out of the back door looking for Pierre. I knew he was somewhere around because we had a shipment coming in and I knew his ass didn't want to miss out on any

product. Tinsley found Pierre in his  apartment upstairs on

the phone. He was in the back room talking, but Tinsley could

hear him from the front door.

"Yea, some fag ass niggas, saying we fucked around in

jail," Pierre advised the person on the phone.

"Yea, nigga named Ryan.  You get the picture I sent you,"

Pierre questioned to the person on the phone. Tinsley listened

in from the other room. She could hear everything Pierre was

saying.  Tinsley was unsure of what the conversation was

about, however she knew Pierre was up to some bullshit.

Tinsley stood behind Pierre's word, but she thought the

situation was handled after Pierre threw Ryan on the floor.

Tinsley decided to barge in on Pierre while he was on the

phone.

"Hey boo," Tinsley stated as she walked in Pierre's back

room. She didn't want Pierre to assume she heard the entire

conversation.  Pierre instantly hung up the phone and responded to Tinsley entering the room.

"What you doing up here," Pierre barked at Tinsley!

"I came up here to check on you," Tinsley replied as she walked toward Pierre.

"Baby, what's wrong with us," Tinsley questioned as she dropped to her knees to expose Pierre's manhood from inside his jeans.

"Tinsley not right now, I have to handle some shit right now," Pierre stated as he pushed Tinsley's head away.

"Why are you pushing me away," Tinsley shouted. Tinsley proceeded to suck on Pierre's tool as she pulled him down to get comfortable in his seat. Tinsley sucked on Pierre's man hood soaking her seamless panties with her juices. She slid her pencil skirt down, leaving her single sole pumps on just in case of a quick escape.  Tinsley stroked Pierre off as she kicked her skirt off. Tinsley sat on Pierre's rod, riding it backwards. She rocked back and forth as Tinsley knew what

Pierre really wanted.  She bent completely over bouncing her ass in front of Pierre's face, sliding up and down as Pierre's legs begin to tense up.  At that very moment Tinsley recognized the appreciation she would never receive from Pierre. She spent years pleasing him in the bedroom and he never returned the favor. She never received oral sex from Pierre and she never asked. She figured he would be willing to please her. The fact that Pierre never took it upon his self, reminded Tinsley that she was the type of woman the needed love and affection. She knew that she wanted to be held. She knew that she was tired of being called her man's bitch when they go out to public places. Tinsley was tired of always pleasing Pierre with sexual pleasure. Even when he was sick, Tinsley felt that sex was the remedy to all. Pierre walked completely over her  He knew he could get away with exactly what he was getting away with, and she'd let him. Everyone in the city knew that Tinsley was Pierre's Bitch, this time Tinsley was fed. She couldn't even see a future for herself because Pierre was standing in the way. She assumed with the quick money he had coming in, Tinsley would be straight. Tinsley knew Pierre loved to show off, and that did mean keeping his lady fly. Tinsley had a sudden urge to grow the hell up. She realized she had a sponsor. Not someone she could spend her life with, start a family an actual man who only gave her financial attention. Hell Tinsley was a PYT.  Older men loved the sight of Tinsley. She always had her cleavage out so they were groping at her rack. Tinsley had a pretty face long hair, and she wore it big with a lot of body. Pierre thrived on that shit. Got the attention of the OG's on the streets. They connected Pierre, because they loved seeing his lady at their parties, and Pierre spent that money.  These older cats had settled own by then. They owned Local bars, motorcycle clubs, diner's you name it. Pierre had excellent connection.  He was trafficking straight through the capital city down to Kentucky to Tennessee. I wasn't mad at his ass.  He was about that cake, and that's the only reason he was around as long as he was.

I left the boutique that night feeling partially satisfied. The sales floor looked fantastic, but I was still waiting on merchandise to arrive. I was so anxious. We had some big wigs coming through, and my mother had been hinting that my grandmother wanted to stop by. My grandmother pretty much let me take completely over. She wasn't one of those controlling women who had to have her nose in everything. She gave me just enough space. There hasn't been an idea of mine yet, that she disagreed with. I guess she was excited to just see the place up and running.

I arrived home and decided to take a hot bath. My body had been aching and that seemed to be the only thing that would help. I started the water and ran it on hot. I poured lavender bath salts into the tub as the aroma filled the bathroom. I melted into the water and spent about 20 minutes in the sauna before my phone rang. I jumped up to answer the phone. Just then I realized it was Toney. I looked at the phone 3 rings before answering.

"Hello," I snapped. I was past irritated assuming he would know to call before close.  I wanted to keep Toney at the boutique, where we can sneak and do us fast quick and easy, here at my place it'll be more intimate, he'll want to stay and be all in my personal space.

"Well Good Evening, my dearest Dionne," Toney stated firm in the most sexiest man voice I have ever heard in my entire life.

"Hello, How are you, why are you calling in so late," I questioned as Toney chuckled in between questions.

"Well Damn Dionne, I didn't know you cared so much, I saw you leave and didn't want to bother you heading home. I didn't want you thinking I was a creep or something. So I waited to call," Toney responded.

Toney's response made all the difference. I was turned on by his ability to strike my interest. He started to become more intriguing with each word he spoke after that. I was past mesmerized. I really wasn't interested in having company but I wanted Toney next to me at that very moment.

"Well that was very gentleman of you," I responded. I grabbed my glass of wine and tilted it back consuming the entire glass in damn near one gulp.

"Baby, you know I'd do anything you want me to, do I hear bath water over there," Questioned Toney.

"Yes, I'm actually taking a hot bubble bath, it's been a long day," I responded.

"Ok, well I didn't want to interrupt, I just wanted to hear your voice," Toney stated as I pulled the phone away and looked at my screen as if he could see me. He completely disregarded the hints I was dropping. Typically a man would immediately take the hint of bathing and ask to come over.

"Well you can stop by if you want, unless you have something else to do," I replied quickly before he hung up the phone.

"Are you sure, I don't want to rush you out of the tub or anything," Toney proclaimed.

"Oh no you're fine, I'll text you my apartment number, and you can just come right on over," I stated as I released the water from the tub.

I couldn't be caught still soaking wet when Toney arrived. I wouldn't make it out of the front room.

## MEANWHILE BACK AT PIERRE'S SPOT

"I don't get it, you break up with me for no apparent reason, and then you don't want to have sex with me, and now you won't even tell me what's going on with you. I'm starting to think maybe Ryan does have some information on you, I feel like you are hiding something from me," Tinsley snapped at Pierre as he ignored her and watched TV as if she wasn't in the room.

"What! You feel like that fag ass nigga got something on me, like what, I don't associate myself with fags, so you want to run that past me one more time," Pierre snarled at Tinsley.

"Listen if you 're going be here, do some work go get in the kitchen and get to whipping, you standing here talking to me like shit goin' change, then sayin' stupid shit about a fag holding info on me," Pierre yelled as Tinsley walked to the kitchen to do exactly what Pierre wanted her to do. Pierre sat on the couch and continued to watch TV as Tinsley slaved away in the kitchen cooking up Pierre's supply. Before there was nothing that would make Tinsley walk away, but now she grew even more frustrated and annoyed by his shit. In Tinsley's mind, she didn't want another bitch all in her man's area, so she made sure Pierre was taken care of even if it did mean sacrificing her own feelings, but with his constant disrespect and violent tone, Tinsley grew enraged, and wanted to bite back, She knew the type of person Pierre was, she didn't want to react out of emotion and start hitting him so she decided to leave silently. It has been years of the same shit. Tinsley

thought about the other females Pierre had been involved with

and realized, Pierre was fucking with her because he loved her

most, he was fucking with her because she was the only stupid

one to stay.

"I'm done with this nigga," Tinsley turned off the stove

and sat the measuring cup and baking soda down. She walked

out of the front door and down the steps back to Pearl.

"Stupid Bitch," Pierre snarled as he ash his black and

mild.


All week, my team and I prepared for our club night

event. Everything seemed to be falling into place just as

planned.  The next morning I woke up to a 7am breakfast and a

note from Toney that read:

Dionne baby,

Look at you resting like a queen. Your bedroom is amazing

I want to sleep here with you forever, as bad as I want to lay in bed with you, I have to get to the office early. I have to make enough money to spoil you once you become mine. Breakfast is served. See you soon.

-Toney

I got dressed neglecting a shower after the intensified sex games I played with Toney the night before. I smelled just like that man. I wanted the smell on me for the rest of the day. He smelled of Dolce Gabbana Men and it was the love passion that had my mind blown.

I arrived at the boutique early that day and hung our newest shipment in the back. I had to make sure our sales floor didn't look empty and we had more than enough merchandise for our customers. The radio had been advertising our event and we also had the DJ from the station stopping in for an hour to show support.

# I'M GAY, NOT CONTAGIOUS

"I can't change who I am. I just wanted you to come to the boutique tonight and see what your son is doing with his life," Isaac proclaimed to his mother as he stood in the kitchen cooking breakfast.

Isaac lived with a roommate whom was also openly gay. They each had men friends. Isaac left home when he was 17 and has lived with the same roommate since. Isaac's mother Louise Dorothy and Father James Dorothy had a 4-bedroom home in Reynoldsburg, Ohio where him and his older twin brother's Antwan and Andrew grew up.

Isaac was a caramel skinned man who kept a fade. He was always tone and fit and was into physical fitness. Growing up, he would condition with the twins during basketball season. After following in the twins footsteps Isaac grew obsessed with staying fit. The twins were also caramel skinned and looked more like their father. They were both over 6 feet and grew out to be more slender than Isaac. Isaac had always felt that the twins were treated better than him. His father worshiped their size 13 feet. They were his all- star college basketball players and he was just a well-kept together prep who had a feminine side. Isaac didn't like getting dirty. He enjoyed talking to his mother in the kitchen while she cooked.

Isaac felt the distance between him and his father in high school. As a freshman Isaac was ranked top 5 in his class. He was always recognized for outstanding grades and performance in the class. He graduated top of his class with honors. Isaac could have gone absolutely anywhere, however he decided to stay in Columbus and attend Columbus School for the Arts. There were honors, banquets and assemblies Isaac was recognized in, but only his mother would come and show support. Isaac supported the twins in majority of all their games and championship games. Isaacc and the twins drifted apart after they moved to New York last year. They started a scholar's camp for young athletes that is actually doing really well.  They do a lot of fitness and conditioning in their

organization that's been recognized throughout the Midwest.

Families have even relocated to send their kids to the program.

Isaac used to host fashion shows all over the city for fashion

designers in school, no one from his family would support him.

He knew early on that his family didn't love him the way that

he felt he should, or the way he loved them.  He stopped

inviting them to events that he was having. In turn he met

friends along the way that shared the same interest and

supported him and pushed him to do better.

"Isaac, I'll have to see what your father says, you know

he doesn't like going to those things," Isaacs Mother shared as

she fried potatoes of the stove.

"What kind of things mom. Look Dionne's grandmother

will be there, so there will be someone there for you. Maybe

you can come alone; this is an adult event, for people who

enjoy fashion. Mom you like fashion, you should come. Hell Dad

doesn't even have to come," Isaac begged.

"Fine, Isaac I will be there. I just don't know how you fell into that lifestyle," Isaac's mother revealed.

"What lifestyle, being a gay man, interested in things that the average male shouldn't be interested in. Well I have news for you Louise Dorothy. We no longer live in the 70's and 80's this is the 20th century. I have the freedom to do exactly what I desire. How can you not accept your own son for who he is? Why is it always a constant battle? Why do I always have to defend liking what I like," screamed Isaac as his mother stood with her back to him, cutting up fruit at the sink.

"I want to support you baby I do, but your father suggest that this is the devils work and it's just a phase in your life that you will overcome," Louise stated.

"Oh ok, so you don't support any of my events? You stop coming to my school functions, because my father says this is the devils work, you leave your son to decide for his self, with no direction and decide to separate yourself. Isaac alleged.

"You Know Isaac, as your mother, I accept you anyhow. My beliefs aren't the same as the ones you've grown accustomed to. I blame myself every day. I don't know where I went wrong with you. Your father kept you in sports; the twins gave you everything you asked for. They loved you Isaac, You were like their triplet. If anything you separated from us. You left the house at seventeen," Louise explained as she turned toward Isaac.

"Mom I left because I didn't feel a part of this family, now your son will be a part of something huge tonight, and I would really like it if you came," Isaac stated in a stern yet calming voice.

Isaac was tired of going back and forth with his mother about how he had been treated his entire childhood. He had joined groups and organizations with other gay men and knew exactly what the struggle between him and his family had been, no matter how his mother wanted to put it. They didn't support gay people. They felt that one of their own turned out to be gay and in turn this is what became of it.

"Mom, I would really love to see your face, I can't change the things that interest me, and I won't apologize for it. It's my lifestyle it's who I am. I do know I need you in my life, supporting me and rooting for me just like you did for the twins," Isaac said one last time before he left his parents' house that day. He had hoped that he got through to his mother and she would show up to show support.

# CLUB NIGHTS

Isaac headed back to the boutique to get ready for the club night event. There were a few designers and vendors coming in to take a peek at Pearl's merchandise. Columbus, Ohio wasn't a fashion capital, but there were a lot of hard working go-getters that deserved to shine. My entire team working for Pearl deserved to be recognized. We all brought something to the table, and that's what I loved most about us. Isaac networked all over the U.S he knew that some of the designers would love to design for pearl. There was even professional stylist that styled celebrities that would be pleased to use Pearl as their number one resource for fashion. Pearl had so much variety, we didn't just aim on club attire, and we had everything from formal, business casual to business.  Depending on how the night went we were going to start our jean line in the winter. We had a manufacture coming in and he also was speaking of partnering with us if he liked what he saw. This night would be huge and beneficial to the rest of our careers. We all anticipated leaving this event with financial gain.

"Mia please this whole entire sales floor needs to be pushed back. We had two movers just standing here a moment ago, if you could just delegate point a finger, something, that would help," I shouted at Mia, as I watched her take a seat on the fashion thrones off to the side of the sales floor. I knew Mia was pregnant, but shit, tonight had to be perfect, I thought.

I had Tinsley taking her shower and getting pretty. To ask of any work from that little heifer would be hell. I hate trying to make Tinsley work, she has a way of making others feel short, or less than. Hell I worked, but I guess we never really worked at the same time I was always the over seer, and Tinsley hated that.

Tinsley shopped in the boutique earlier that day, I allowed them two items in the store as a gift from me. They deserved it. Even if at times they became difficult to deal with, they deserved it. One of my good friends Cheyenne who had been doing my hair since my senior year in high school had already come in to set up. Tinsley got her hair done, her face was beat to perfection, and she was just being a superior princess all day.  Getting on everyone's nerve. I let her do exactly what she wanted to do. It was the best way to keep the drama down. My sisters also each had a copy of my key.  So if they ever needed to get to my apartment and I'm unavailable they have that option.

I walked around the boutique making sure everything was up to my standard. We closed the doors two hours prior to the event for last minute survey. I decided to head back to my office, I had been thinking about massaging my feet with my spa chair I recently ordered. Justine went home for a nap, Isaac and Mia went to my apartment and I had assumed Tinsley did the same. I hit the lights and watched the scented candles on top of the antique cupboards illuminate my grandmother's store.  I walked in my office and turned the fish tank lights on. I noticed Toney sitting on the arm of my guest couch with a bouquet of white roses. One of the biggest grins I've ever known of, erupted on my face.

"Hi handsome," I stated, as I reached in for a hug.

Toney placed the flowers down beside him and reached in to grab my ass. He pulled me in so tight if I wanted to run from him I would get an Indian burn. That man was so fine. I think that's why I played with his emotions the way I did. He was everything, if I wanted to settle, Anthony Reginald Cox would come to mind.

"Hey beautiful, I've been thinking about you all day," Toney stated as he grabbed my face in for a kiss.

Toney stood to his feet towering over my body, continuing to grab my lower back his Dolce cologne removed my soul. He looked so relieved to see me. We stood in complete silence hugging one another. I felt so safe standing there, and I could tell I was the stress ball he's been waiting to squeeze on.

"Babe you're just in time," I shouted as I immediately stopped my words from flowing. I smiled because calling Toney babe felt so right.

"Really, well what was the Lovely Dionne Simone about to do," Toney stated as he smiled and turned around toward my spa-chair in the corner of my office.

Toney was one of the few people that understood my office was my first home. I only had an apartment because it was the only normal thing to do. The bathroom in my office made it nearly impossible to ever leave.

"Well considering that fact that you've been running through my mind all day, your feet must be wore out and in need of some attention," Toney chuckled as he turned the of the footbath. I climbed in the chair and hiked up my skirt.

"Toney, why don't you come up here with me," I suggested as I reached for his hand.

"The chair is big enough for both of us. " I assured Toney as he took off his shoes then socks. I looked down smiling just so he could have the notion I like man feet.

I stood up allowing Toney to sit in the chair only leaving me the opportunity to sit on his lap. Toney grabbed me tight around my waist and we watched the footbath fill up with bubbles. The warm water soaked our feet as the jets shooting from the sides washed away the day's stress.

"I could do this every day with you," I reveled. "Well what are we waiting for exactly? Why do you shoot me down? I'm giving you all the signs. You think I would waste my time with someone I wasn't interested in," Toney argued. "It's hard to tell, I mean you're a guy. Isn't that what guys do. Take for granted women that are giving you what you want," I questioned. Hell I had my doubts too. I wasn't crazy for turning down a good man. They trick us, and they come with baby faces saying all of the right things with warm hands and big arms. Just like my Toney.

"You know what I'll give you that, but baby I've financially invested in you long before you were giving me anything extra, so I should've gotten recognition simply because of that. You know in the back of your mind, Toney got you don't you," Toney grilled.

"Yes, that's right, you spent numerous nights with me, just keeping me company so I wouldn't be here by myself, "I replied.

Toney was right. Maybe I was the one emotionally detached. Toney was a friend to me. I felt absolutely no pressure from him. I had decided to go for it. If it didn't work he can't say I didn't try.

I bent down to turn the knobs off, the tub had filled to our liking and I only wanted to savor the moment. I leaned back one hundred percent sure of my next move.

"Toney, I want to take you out, spend a whole day with you, I want you to be my man," I proclaimed. Toney lit up like a light bulb. He smiled and started nibbling on my ear.

"I can do that for you," Toney whispered.

I stepped down from the spa chair. Toney followed me. I took my hair down from the high bun I had adjusted to perfection this morning for work. Toney unbuttoned his shirt. I opened my office door and walked out toward the sales floor to make sure the front doors were locked. I walked to the front door and didn't see anything.

Just then I could feel Toney breathing down the back of my neck. He circled his fingers around my belly button and down the front of my seamless panties. I could feel my sweet juices springing from my box. Toney pushed me onto the mannequin stand and dove in headfirst. The streets were silent and the store was dark, but if someone stopped in front of the window they could see me enjoying the best oral satisfaction brought to me by mankind. Toney pushed me back and submerged his entire face into my honey pot. Toney sucked up the sweetest nectar and forced his fingers up my vaginal passage. I climaxed numerous times moaning Toney's name as if he stopped and disappeared into thin air. Toney came up for air and almost in an instant I grabbed his manhood and shoved it into my box. I needed to feel his rod sliding in and out of me. The magnitude of my hormones had reached an entire new level. Toney pushed me up against the front entrance doorframe and I wrapped my legs around him and erupted all on his Johnson. I could feel Toney swell up and gripped my ass so tight I thought he would rip my ass cheeks apart.

"Dionne I want to cum inside of you," Toney moaned as his strokes became harder and faster.

"You can cum inside of me baby, I yelled as Toney exploded inside of me. His tensed up muscles released, and I could feel the hot steam turn into cold sweat. We both stood to our feet and scurried back to my office. I had a shower in my office and already had my evening attire there. I shut the door and locked it behind me. I walked toward my bathroom and started up a shower to finish what we started. I knew Toney and I weren't finished. Toney followed me to the bathroom and

shut the door behind him.

# Collateral

"Listen just meet me there, 3am tonight. We're having an event that ends at 1am so I will be there late. Smooth transaction. No one would even know," Justine explained while writing down the combinations to both safes in the store.

Justine was my financial backbone. Even though this was my boutique, Justine had a minor in accounting when she was in college. I trusted her with every cent that came into the store. We had a system, so there was no way she could short change me without taking full responsibility. I went to the bank every morning to deposit the previous day's profit, no matter the dollar amount. Even if Justine didn't work that day, she is responsible for following up with the store every night to ensure the closing amount.

"I just got dressed and I'm heading there now," Explained Justine as she wrapped up her conversation on the phone.

"So tired of not getting my bonuses. I've made this damn boutique my priority. All of the side money coming in here, and I can't get a monetary thank you, I'm not playing this go around. I'm going to get my cut," Justine said aloud to herself as she drove to the boutique for the club night event.

"Dionne walks around like everyone owes her something while her sisters run around doing whatever the fuck they want. No type of structure at all. Just a bunch of messy bitches," Justine encouraged herself as she grew more and more anxious about what she had planned.

Justine knew her position at the boutique. She knew that we depended on her a lot. She was a huge part that was holding us together. I had an enormous amount of respect for her. Matter of fact, she got paid almost as much as me. She was on salary and we had it in the budget to pay her 80,000 a year. In addition to her blog that she had up and running which was doing wonderful. I trusted her, and my grandmother did too.

Anything extra, I couldn't put her in on. She talked to damn much. Hell, I was messy for doing it right under her nose. I knew Justine didn't give a fuck about nobody but her damn self.

Justine arrived back at the boutique as normal. I didn't hear her come in because I was in my office with toney getting ready for the night. The back door was open and Justine came right in. Justine could see all the lights still off so she went into the meeting room because she could see my office door still shut.  Justine reached for her phone and just then heard the back door shut. She turned around startled and afraid to see who was behind her. When she turned toward the door she realized Wayne was standing in the doorway.

"Oh hey Wayne, you looking for Mia," Justine questioned annoyed with all the infidelity that was going on around her.

Justine was so emotionally drained. She had been open to dating and unable to find a mate because of her excessive late nights and dedication to Pearl.  It was as if everyone around her were in a dysfunctional relationship. She knew she could do better by a man than any of the other women could.

"Yea they left to get dressed for the night, I'm actually unsure what time they would be back," Justine confirmed.

"Well I guess I'll stay right here until she gets back," Wayne suggested as he sat down in the chair next to Justine and crossed his arms.

"Ok, but typically Dionne doesn't allow non-employee's back here, but I'll tell her you're waiting for Mia," Justine completed.

"Oh ok, that'll work," Wayne stated.

"So you still haven't got a hold of Mia since the last time you were here," Justine questioned in confusion.

Justine began to wonder what the holdup was. Mia was out of her mind to play a man like Wayne. He worshiped the ground she walked on and someone needed to show her man what he was worth.

"You know, I heard her talking to Dionne, and she told me all about the secret get away you guys had in Chicago that day. No wonder you were looking for her. Did you guys get in to it, is that the reason she's avoiding you," Justine blurted out.

Justine knew in her heart that Mia was not in Chicago with Wayne. In fact she knew that Mia was laid up with a man she had no business being laid up with. Wayne instantly grew infuriated and in response asked Justine if she wanted to sit on his lap. Justine sought out any opportunity for revenge and went for it. She sat on Wayne's lap and spoke encouraging words to him.

"That wasn't you, in Chicago was it," Justine questioned, knowingly aware of the answer.

"No, It wasn't, you know this for sure, that Mia was with someone," Wayne confirmed.

"Well I walked in Dionne's office when Dionne asked where she was and she said she had been at a hotel in Chicago, I assumed it was you," Justine confirmed.

Wayne leaned in to kiss Justine. All of his anger somehow turned into sexual revenge. He became overly aggressive in pleasing Justine, and she was more than willing. Wayne unbuttoned Justine's blouse and he began sucking on her nipples as she gripped the back of Wayne's head. Wayne had pulled his manhood out of his pants exposing his full erect penis. Justine grabbed his rod and began stroking it.

"Wayne you deserve a woman that will stroke you every single night," Justine persuaded.

Wayne began kissing on Justine's neck. Giving her all of the male attention she had been missing these last few months. Justine's ex-boyfriend cheated on her the entire two years they were together. The woman he cheated on Justine for, ended up pregnant and they got married. Justine gave up on love and became bitter that all men were the same.

"Jump on, I want to take you for a ride," Wayne encouraged as Justine continued to stroke him.

"Right here, right now," Justine questioned, as she stood to her feet ready for what was expected from Wayne.

"Yea, right now, what better time than the one that exist," Wayne insisted.

Justine decided to go for what was in front of her. Never mind the fact the she was dressed in a $1,300 cocktail dress. She pulled her dress up exposing her ladybug tattoo imprinted on her ass outlined by her silk thong. Wayne inserted his fingers into Justine's gushing juices. Wayne slid his erect penis inside of Justine. Justine slid comfortably down Wayne's rod lubricating him with her womanly fluids. Wayne stood to his feet and pulled away from Justine as she backed up threshing his pelvis.

"Turn around," Wayne stated as he assisted Justine on top of the conference table.

Justine backed up onto the table leaning back. She pulled Wayne in and on top of her. At this tempting point they both neglected contraceptive, and the chance of someone walking in on them. Wayne began gripping Justine's breast as he rammed his love muscle inside of her. Justine indulged into the moment that existed. At that very moment she had surrendered herself as the villain. Justine's brown skin toned kissed Wayne's caramel bicep's as he pulled Justine's thigh's in to meet his over and over Wayne pulled in and out to reach his highest potential climax. He then grabs Justine's neck and corkscrew her vaginal hole. Justine's let off two faint moans gearing up Wayne's ego. Over and over Wayne pumped faster and faster, just then Justine pushes Wayne to the ground kissing him and going down his stomach and onto his penis. Justine grabbed held of Wayne and shoved almost 8 inches of him into her mouth. She soaked Wayne's rod with Saliva as she slurped his helmet while he ignited his bodily fluids into Justine's mouth. Meanwhile Justine had her left hand caressing her clitoris, while squirting and soaking the floor. Wayne grabbed the back of Justine's head as he stood to his feet fucking her face. Justine gripped on tight and did not stop. Just then Justine slurped up her mess and spit it onto the conference room floor. Wayne pushed Justine back onto the conference table and dove in for one more lap.

See after hearing all of this went down, I now know that women thrive off of emotion. Whatever the motive may be, there is emotion behind it. They give themselves up. Justine knew very well that she would never be with Wayne, but she also knew she would never be able to label the the Bradly sisters including Mia as friends. Mia and Justine may have not been the best of friends, but all lines were crossed. They were co-workers, and Justine had given up information that should have been kept to herself. In that very an instant, Justine had become the other woman. My sister comes first regardless of business. Do I take a step back and reevaluate the situation. Yes! But dammit, I'd beat the pope's ass if he crossed my family.

Tinsley entered the boutique from the back door. She had been at Dionne's apartment getting dressed with Mia and

Isaac. She decided to arrive at the boutique a little early. A few

of the hairstylist had called her and advised that they would be

heading back soon and Dionne wasn't answering her phone.

When Tinsley arrived she noticed the lights off on the show

floor, but could see candles burning. She noticed all the

backroom doors were shut. Tinsley assumed they were

occupied so she headed straight for the conference room. This

was the only common area in the store where everyone had

authority. Once she grabbed the handle she could hear

slapping and soft moaning. Tinsley crept in anyway.  The lights

were off, however the lights from the television screens

mounted on the walls were well lit. Wayne and Justine were in

the spotlight in the center of the conference room table. Tinsley

grabbed her phone and begin recording what she saw. She

wanted proof. She knew that Justine would deny what she did

and so would Wayne.  Tinsley softly shut the door and turned

to Dionne's office door to find that it was locked. Dionne could

hear giggling so she decided to knock anyway.

"Dionne open up, it's me," Tinsley shouted as she banged on Dionne's office door.

"What in the hell, why are you banging so hard," Dionne stated as she flung open her office door still smiling and flirting with Toney.

Tinsley walked into Dionne's office in a panic, still watching the video she just recorded, pissed at what she just witnessed.

"We need to call Mia, she needs to get here now," Tinsley stated frantic, as she entered the room.

"Well why don't you call her, what's wrong," Dionne questioned confused.

"Dionne why the hell did I just see... Tinsley slowed down her words as she spotted Toney walking out of my bathroom buttoning his shirt.

"Oh, sorry, I didn't realize you had company," Tinsley stated.

"No you're fine, Toney this is my little sister Tinsley, Tinsley this is Toney, he'll be joining us tonight," I proclaimed as I sat down on the couch to buckle my shoe.

"Look at this shit, Tinsley stated as she put her phone in Dionne's face while playing the video of Justine and Wayne.

"Wow, on my conference table tho," Dionne stated in jealousy, as she realized she wasn't the only one fucking on the conference table.

"But who is the guy, he looks like Wayne," Dionne brushed off as she handed the phone back to Tinsley.

"Girl that is Wayne, look closer," Tinsley confirmed as she zoomed in on the video.

"What, is he here, where the hell is Mia, This is happening right now," Dionne stated more concerned after putting everything into perspective.

"Oh, hell no," Dionne stood to her feet and stormed toward the door.

"Listen, Dionne no, we have to go about this very strategic. I'm more concerned about this night going up in flames because we drag your financial advisor out of this boutique by her hair. We have the proof let's speak to Mia and see how she wants to handle it," Tinsley suggested.

She was right. Tinsley was always the one getting into shit, this time she had to be the bigger person. She knew I felt crossed. Though she couldn't wait to put her hands on Justine she finally wanted to be there for her sister's the way we had been there for her.  The separation between her and Pierre made her think of how lucky and blessed she truly was. She has a family that protects her, and she wanted to do the same for them. She got her emotions under control the moment she recorded that video. That was all the proof necessary to get Justine the fuck up out of Pearl.

"Dionne, you have to hold it together. We will explain this to Mia as soon as we get the opportunity. That bitch isn't getting away with this," Tinsley assured as she wiped tears from Dionne's face.

Toney walked toward me concerned that this night would be ruined. He knew I took pride in my work, and that I was also crazy about my sisters.

"Listen, Dionne, you may not trust me to take control, but I got your back, you've always been here for me and I'm going to step up tonight. You stay back here, get yourself together and I'll go host until you're ready. I won't let you down, I know what this night means to you," Tinsley confirmed as she took the leadership role this time, taking the pressure off of Dionne.

Tinsley felt that I worked hard my entire life, never asking anyone for anything, therefore she wanted to put me on a slight pedal stool during the time I needed it most. I grew an abundance of respect for her that night.

"Okay Tinsley, You know the motto, "

"It's Business Baby," They decreed in unison.

"I'm trusting you, Me Me Priss is coming and this is her throne, if anything goes wrong..."

"I know, I know," Tinsley interrupted.

"It's taken care of. Toney nice meeting you, I know it's a lot of trust issues going on right now, but I'm trusting you with my sister tonight," Tinsley declared.

It was nearly time for the club night event to start. All hairstylist and makeup personal had guaranteed a return time of two hours from the time of equipment drop off. Everyone was expected back at any moment. Tinsley decided to leave Dionne alone with Toney, she knew her sister had a lot at steak and the last thing Dionne needed was emotions in the way of business.

Tinsley headed back out toward the sales floor. She noticed the conference room door cracked open. She could see Wayne sitting in a chair texting on his phone; he wore sweatpants and a tee shirt looking sweaty and hot.

"I can't believe this nigga, its lights out for this bastard," Tinsley said under her breath as she walked past the door. She could see Wayne lift his head as he heard someone in the hallway.

"Oh Hey Justine, have you opened the doors yet," Tinsley quizzed, as she walked back onto the show room floor.

Justine put me in such a compromising place; she would have no choice but to get picked on by the most territorial person in my family. Tinsley!

This woman was well trusted; she held the financial key to this store. She carried all of the resources to profiting and providing exemplary employee benefits. After tonight we wouldn't need her resources anyway," Tinsley thought.

Tinsley wanted to get down to business. Justine not only crossed Mia as a co-worker but me as a friend and Tinsley wasn't going for that. I knew Tinsley was going to fuck with her the moment she left my office. But see I felt if the bitch was bold enough to do some cold hearted shit like that then the bitch could hold her own.

I knew that Justine's financial plan was a successful one. That's actually what hurt me the most. Justine was someone I'd go to for business advice. She has always been a good friend to me. I know Tinsley felt there was a way to handle this, and even though I didn't trust Tinsley, I had a gut instinct she was going to step up to the plate.  Pearl's motto has always been all about business, and I know for a fact Tinsley respected it. That saying came directly out of the ruler's mouth. Me Me Priss didn't play when it came to Pearl. We had no choice but to keep business priority.  However this time one of our own had been crossed and that actually came right before business. Family was first, can't forget to mention we had an employee of Pearl in the conference room of the boutique having sex. This is automatic termination. Justine thought she had one up on us, but she was gone, which was already established before I walked out of that office door that night. Right after she brought in her old colleagues' as promised, Justine would be dismissed.

"Uhm actually, the event starts at 7pm, its only 6:49 I'll open them in just a moment," Justine confirmed as she went through tonight's reservations.

"Smart ass. I couldn't even start with her tonight. She can use whatever smart ass antics she likes. I'm getting ready to mind fuck her. Use what I know against her. Considering the fact that Wayne is still here, only means he's trying to stick around for Mia, Tinsley thought to herself.

Tinsley walked to the back, to see what Wayne was doing in the conference room. She walked in and noticed him talking on his phone. Tinsley couldn't make out what Wayne was discussing but Tinsley made it known that she was standing in the room.

"Hey Wayne," Tinsley stated as Wayne turned to face Tinsley square in the eye.

"Hello Tinsley, how are you," Asked Wayne.

"I'm good just wanted to speak with you for a brief moment," Tinsley stated as she closed the door.

Wayne instantly got nervous. He was unsure what this talk would be about, but considering the fact that he just had Justine all over the conference table, he had plenty to be scared of. This was something different. This was something that would benefit tonight's event. Tinsley needed to make sure Wayne was out of the way. He clearly came for trouble. Just last week Mia was the woman you wanted to marry and now this week you have her co-worker bent over at her job. Mia had some secrets too but they weren't messy and compromising the family business.

"We're a little short staff, I know you're here for Mia, but she'll be working too. I figured we could all come together and work as a team. After all, you're about to marry my sister, may as well join the family business," Tinsley mislead.

Wayne shook his head in agreement. He wanted nothing more than for Mia to notice him being there for her. If this would get him closer to her, Wayne was willing to do it.

"Ok so what do you want me to do," Wayne asked.

"Valet parking. He doesn't have a second person to valet the cars, the attendant is outside but he needs a runner. Would you be willing to help out," Tinsley asked as she smiled trying to persuade Wayne that helping out would be a good idea.

"Ok, I'll do it, it can't be that hard," Wayne agreed as he started to walk toward the door.

"Just stay here, I have something you can put on," Tinsley stated as she walked out of the conference room and into the back stock room to grab a Pearl logo polo shirt and men's slacks.

"I can't believe we actually have stuff back here for him to put on. This works, he'll really feel like he's official," Tinsley chuckled aloud.

Tinsley walked back to the conference room and gave Wayne the clothes she had retrieved from the back stock room. Tinsley shut the door of the conference room and heard Mia walk in talking to Justine.

"What did you get to eat," Mia stated to Justine as she showed her the bag to Stephanie's an Italian grill that Justine, Mia and I often went to for lunch.

"Mia, honey, come here," Tinsley interrupted as Justine looked in Tinsley's direction.

Justine knew that Tinsley was in the conference room talking to Wayne. She was unsure about what, but the plan was to put Justine in complete discomfort. So fuck what she thought.

Mia walked toward Tinsley and Isaac walked toward the dressing room transformed hair station's to look at the set up's. The hair stylist were finishing up and preparing for the night.

Justine grew very uncomfortable and couldn't help the heat that she felt as she listened to Tinsley whispering to Mia. Justine quickly disrupted their conversation to see if she could sense any womanly hostility.

"Ok girls it's that time, everyone get prepared," Justine stated as she walked to the entrance doors to unlock them.

Tinsley decided to ignore Justine's willingness to get everyone excited about the club night event coming to the boutique. Tinsley felt Justine was nervous she couldn't be too candid tonight. She felt under pressure and more than likely stay out of the way of trouble.  Tinsley grabbed Mia's shoulders and looked her square in the eye.

"Well you look amazing," Tinsley said to Mia pulling her in for a hug.

"Thank you, I was feeling real down about seeing Lamont in Chicago, so I wanted to look extra gorgeous when

Wayne came looking for me tonight. No way he would tell me

No in this dress," Mia expressed.

"Actually Wayne is already here. He's going to be

running for Valet tonight," Tinsley communicated to Mia.

"Why is he running for valet," Mia questioned.

"He wanted to help out," Tinsley ensured. She didn't

want to reveal too much information before Mia acted on

emotions and erupted all over Justine's ass.

"That's odd," Mia stated.

"Well he was here and we needed the help so he

agreed," Tinsley shared with Mia.

Mia would only hear the bare minimum. This night

needed to run smooth and Tinsley was in charge of that. She

felt like for once she had the entire boutique in her hands, and

what better night, than the night Me Me Priss and our parents

would be stopping by. Justine thought for certain that she was

running things tonight. Business was the motive, so I could tell

Tinsley allowed her to entertain her invited guest and that was it.

The girls watched as shoppers who had appointments come in and get their hair done, get makeup done and shopped for the evening's festivities. We even brought in our seasonal employees for this event. They were in school for fashion merchandising and agreed to come to the boutique to help out with the event.

An hour had flown by once I noticed Dionne hadn't come out of her office. I looked around and noticed everything going pretty steady. People were enjoying themselves, laughing and talking.

Tinsley was very much aware that my mother, stepfather, and grandmother were scheduled to arrive at any moment. If anything, I know she would take credit for everything going smooth so she would make sure the night was satisfactory.

"Dionne, open up it's me," I knocked on the door.

Toney opened the door and invited me in; I walked in and noticed Dionne sitting on the edge of her desk.

"Well, what you are doing, a lot of people are asking about you. Me Me Priss Mother, and Mr. Ray will be here any minute you do realize that right? They can't see you crying, chop chop" Tinsley teased.

"Your sister is a bit frustrated," Toney advised as he rubbed my back for comfort.

Tinsley looked me in the face and noticed I had been crying.

"Damn what the hell Dionne, don't worry about it, everything is going to be ok," Tinsley assured me.

"I'm coming I just needed a moment to get my mind together. I don't understand why Justine would do this tonight of all nights Tinsley. This makes me feel weird. Did Mia do something to her? I just don't get it," I shouted, in complete astonishment. I'm coming I have some designers coming that want to partner with us and I need to be focused. Give me a few more minutes. I insisted.

Tinsley walked out of my office. She knew I would take this situation completely personal. I loved Justine. I fought for her to work for Pearl. Tinsley was actually the one always putting her down and saying that Justine was shifty. So you have to understand, this was really getting to me.

Tinsley walked on the sales floor and noticed our two seasonal employees, Shayla and Jasmine checking in on our guest. Everything seemed to be running smoothly.

Just then Tinsley watched Toney and I come from the back.

"Hello everyone," I shouted as she grabbed Toney's hand.

"I want to thank everyone for coming out tonight. Hopefully you all find what you're looking for. We are here to get you ready for tonight, so hopefully we will go above and beyond to meet those expectations for you.

Everyone clapped for me after I was done speaking. I was well known around the city.  Everyone had heard about the club night event and was anxious to see what was in store for the night. We had the DJ from one of the radio stations here in Columbus, they agreed to record live while at the event to help promote. So many guests stopped in after hearing him.

"Isaac can I talk to you," I stated to Isaac as I interrupted him being silly in front of his friends.

"Hey what's goin' on D," Isaac stated taking another sip of Champaign.

"We're doing really good tonight. We were able to bring in $34,000 tonight so far. Not including our service packages. I need you to handle the money after closing. We'll put it in the back up safe and go to the bank in the morning" I advised Isaac.

"Well I'll ask Justine to help, she's good with counting down the store," Isaac expressed.

"You know what, Justine will be in my office at that time. I don't want her fingers on another dollar from Pearl," Dionne suggested.

Isaac raised his eyebrows, at the sudden distaste for Justine touching the money. Everyone knew Justine was over the money. Something was going on and Isaac grew curious. He didn't want to ask Dionne because her mind seemed to be made up. He decided to try and get the information from Mia. Isaac walked away and headed straight toward Mia as she sat in the royalty chairs in the corner of the store on her phone.

"Hey mom, it's me Mia, I checked your itinerary and noticed you didn't board your flight, just want to make sure everything is okay, call me and let me know," Mia communicated with her mother on her cell phone

Mia had invited her mother and purchased her flight so that she could also be a part of Pearl's event. Everyone was in town and Mia wanted her mother to be apart.

Issac walked over to Mia unconcerned about who she was on the phone with and interrupted her phone conversation.

"So what the hell is going on with your sister and Justine," Isaac questioned assuming Mia knew exactly what was going on.

"I don't know, she didn't tell me anything," Mia advised.

"Yea, Dionne told me to count down the store tonight, she said she didn't want Justine near another dollar inside of Pearl after tonight," Isaac said to Mia.

"That's weird, I don't know, we'll have to find out once we close," Mia suggested.

Meanwhile Justine introduced all of her sponsors and investors to me.

I knew that with everything that was going on under the table I had to make quite the impression on the investors, so they wouldn't need Justine as a middleman anymore. I spoke with William Sheldon. Who owns Lace Line, a well-known women's lingerie store inside of Columbus's downtown mall. He spoke with me about partnering with Pearl for a percentage in sales if he sold a few pieces of his merchandise in Pearl. We exchanged information, and instantly became acquaintances.

I was on a mission to get to everyone that Justine brought in that night. I was so furious with her; I couldn't let those feelings show. Everyone that was beneficial to Pearl had my contact information. I had to pretend that nothing was bothering me the whole time I spoke with Justine. I knew at that very moment we had to resolve this issue before leaving the boutique. I never thought of replacing her. Justine without a doubt made sure we ran smooth.

Just then I noticed a black Lincoln town car pulling up to valet. The car parked and I noticed my mother appear from the back seat.

"Mia, Tinsley, they're here," I shouted across the show room floor.

I watched my stepfather help my grandmother out of the car and head in our direction. We all gathered around the door, to welcome them with gratitude. No matter how much money we made, this is where we came from. These were the individuals who invested in us the most. Just then Me Me Priss, Mr. Ray and our mother walked into the boutique greeted with hugs and handclaps. They soaked up the entrance they just made. We made sure whenever they came around they were treated like royalty. All you could see was a huge smile permanently placed on Me Me Priss' face once she entered the store.

"Mom, look at you, I stated as I grabbed my mother in for a hug.

"Well you know, I had this gown I've been dying to wear, and I thought what better event than the girls'," Eileen advised.

"Me Me Priss, who styled you, you look amazing," I shouted, teasing my grandmother. I had a dress made especially for her to wear that night.

"Oh child, stop," My grandmother brushed off as she tried pulling Tinsley's gown together. Tinsley's cleavage was bulging out of her dress and my grandmother hated seeing our breasts out.

"Well Hey Mr. Ray, you look good as well, how was your trip, I asked.

"It was alright, would have been much better if your grandmother wouldn't have called the entire time we were on the road. She didn't stop until we picked her up," Mr. Ray stated chuckling.

Mr. Ray wasn't a man of many words but he supported us. He was always there smiling and enjoying his self. He just blended in no matter where he was. I had our server's make my family some drinks and returned to my guest I watched Mia and Tinsley entertaining them so I knew they would be ok. It was always a joy seeing my family. My grandmother admired the store as she grabbed each piece of merchandise on the show room floor. I watched as she showed my mother the chandelier that hung in the center of the show room. I was pleased as I watched everyone admire our work and efforts. I watched Mia and Mr. Ray escape to the opposite side of the boutique to converse amongst each other.

"Hey dad, I sent mom a flight, and I checked her itinerary this morning and even about an hour ago and she never checked in to board the plane.  Did she contact you on why she wasn't coming," Mia stated confused as to why her mother neglected to contact her about her whereabouts or any explanation as to why she didn't board the plane and she said that she would.

"Mia baby, I have not spoken to your mother, I don't remember the last time we had a decent conversation," Mr. Ray advised Mia.

"Listen sweet heart your mother is probably busy, now what she's doing I'm unsure of, but I'm sure once you leave a message she'll call you back," Mr. Ray confirmed as he kissed

Mia on the cheek and walked back over toward Tinsley and his wife.

Mia soaked in her disappointment. Mia's grandmother's phone had been disconnected for a few months and her mother never returned her phone calls. Mia hated that thought of losing touch with her mother. Mia has always reached out to her mother and her mother used to call in to check on her from time to time but in her more recent years, they calls became shorter and shorter.

As I noticed Mia disappear to the back, I watched a familiar face walk through the door. I wasn't sure who the gentleman was but he looked vaguely familiar.

"Isaac, I called out, could you assist this gentleman, he looks like he may be looking for something," I called out as I looked in the direction of the unfamiliar face.

I found Toney in the corner of the room chit chatting with a few of the investors Justine had invited. As Toney led the conversation between the colleagues that Justine invited, I instantly became comfortable. All that I was really doing was looking pretty. Toney had it under control. He spoke of Pearl as if he has been helping me run it the entire time. I could definitely tell that Justine was a bit uncomfortable.

"Hey honey," Toney stated as he pulled me in for a hug.

"I just wanted to come over and check on you," I explained as I smiled and nodded at each of the gentlemen standing in the small circle.

It seems that Toney had his own entertainment going on. He had made friends and it seemed that they had a lot in common, as I noticed them all with the same drink.

"Well you are actually just in time. This is Mike, Stanley, James and Bennett," Toney introduced as I shook each of their hands.

"We all had mutual friends in college and they were invited by Justine," Toney shared, as he looked me in the eye confirming that he's already in good with these investors.

I asked if they were enjoying themselves and could tell that Toney had this one in the bag. This was all the confirmation that I needed. I could tell that he had my back as I turned around and noticed all of the men looking in my direction.

"Dionne, hey yes we need you over here for just a moment," Isaac pulled me away from the conversation I was having with the private investors.

"Well Damn I was kind of in the middle of something," I proclaimed as I struggled to escape Isaacs grip.

Isaac pulled me over to the gentlemen that I just asked him to assist.

"Hello," I greeted as I shook the gentleman's hand.

"Hello, Dionne do you remember me," The man questioned.

"Well you do look familiar, can't say that I remember your name though," I advised.

"I'm Lamont I'm good friends of Mia's. We hung out back in Chicago," The man shared as he watched my eyes grow bigger than my face would allow.

"I decided to drive down after Mia told me about the event. I definitely wanted to show my support. I'm really impressed, you ladies are doing a great job as I can see," Lamont established as he looked around at the antique cabinets and   merchandise that filled the store.

"Well you can make yourself comfortable, Mia will be out in just a moment," I advised Lamont as he walked to the mini bar for a drink.

Just then I spotted Mia walking from the back. She looked like she had a lot on her mind so I didn't want to startle her but I did want to make her aware that the man she crept around with back home, had drove all the way here just to see her.

"Mia honey, hey, Uhm the guy you were with in Chicago is here, Lamont right," I questioned Mia as I watched her body tense up.

"Where is he, he can't be here, Wayne is here, if he finds out who he is, he will kill him," Mia stated startled that Wayne would put two and two together.

I was more worried that Justine would find out what's going on and try to be shifty. Mia knew nothing of the infidelity between her boyfriend and Justine. I wanted to make sure that no one was trying to sabotage this event any further.

"Mia just go say Hi you know, show him around, and send him on his way,"

In an instant I grew infuriated all over again. Lamont needed to go, and not because I didn't like him or anything, but because If Wayne found out what was going on in the party, I'd possibly have to put a bullet in him. The soft ones were the crazy ones, and the way he was trying to control his relationship, I could tell he'd try it tonight.

I noticed Mia taking Lamont toward the back. With everything Tinsley had explained, Justine was the cooperate tonight. She seemed to be the only one trying to fuck up my money.  I decided to go chat with her to take her eyes off of any interesting movement she may have spotted with her nosey ass.

"Amazing turn out tonight, we did it Justine. We're making progress just like you said we would," I advised Justine as she smiled at me.

"We did didn't we," Justine responded short and dry.

Justine always added her input after her answer. This time she gave the bare minimum. Justine had every right to feel uncomfortable that night. Her conscious was eating at her, and that was all the proof I needed that she had unknowingly become an enemy and untrustworthy. A real friend would patch up their wrongs right away. No matter how guilty and how wrong. We all make mistakes. Justine however seemed as if she wanted to stay in that place. A place of uncertainty, and ambiguity. With me that was a fucked up place to be. Tinsley

spotted Justine and I exchanging words. Once she and I made

eye contact, I knew her nosey ass would make her way over.

"Hey Dionne, look at Pearl girl, you did it," Dionne stated

sarcastic.

I could tell she wanted to exclude Justine from and

praises and glory given to Pearl that night. It was steaming up.

Tinsley was on a roll and actually had the power to shit on

Justine's entire existence.

"If it wasn't for you I don't think tonight would have

been a success," Tinsley added.

I watched Justine squirm in her skin as Tinsley

made it her personal mission to uncover Justine's

malicious personality.

"Where is Mia, Mr. Ray is looking for her,"

Tinsley questioned as she scanned the room for Mia.

"She's in my office on the phone," I fabricated to

Tinsley.

Tinsley made her way to the back room to find Tinsley. She opened my office door and noticed Tinsley and Lamont talking on my office couch.

"Oh I'm sorry, I didn't know you were busy, I need to see you when you're done," Tinsley specified as she shut my office door, leaving Mia and Lamont to their privacy.

"That was Tinsley right," Lamont questioned Mia as he looked toward the door.

"Yea that's her she may have not recognized you, otherwise she would have said hi," Mia assured as she finished her statement that Tinsley interrupted by bursting in.

"Mia, I was pissed you left me in that room like that. Our first time? I thought we shared something that night. I mean, damn ma, I didn't know you got down like that. You always took me as the wholesome type, but you banged out," Lamont confessed as he shook his head side eyeing Mia.

Mia was a bit confused on why Lamont showed up. She did mention it and left the flyer on the dresser that night but she was just showing off the boutique's success. She had no idea that he was going to actually show up. Mia was someone different the night she and Lamont hooked up. He was her escape. He embraced everything about her that night. He took pride on being able to capture the attention of someone so intellectual and striking. Mia had it all and she broke his heart with one snap.

"I know but," Mia stopped in the middle of her statement.  She wanted to create a fairy tale that only existed in her world, but she decided to tell Lamont the truth. The very thing that had been overpowering her.

"Listen Lamont, I don't want to create any more of a disaster than I already have, so I definitely want to be honest, Wayne and I are still involved. We were going through a really rough time when we meet up back in Chicago," Mia started.

"I was aware, I know you had your thing with him, but Mia that ain't got shit to do with me," Lamont interrupted.

Mia could easily identify the arrogant tone Lamont was letting off. She decided not to go against him and let him have his say.

"Ok, well you didn't know I was pregnant," Mia finished as she forced her way through Lamont's mumbles.

Lamont stopped his words and chuckled. "Damn Mia, you're just full of surprises tonight huh," Lamont urged.

"I'm sorry, I didn't mean for it to happen this way," Mia shouted over top of Lamont's emotions that were screaming through his eyeballs.

Lamont was passed pissed. He started to remove his self from the room, but his feet wouldn't let him move. Mia became nervous at the thought of losing Lamont as a friend because of her bad decisions. She decided to explain only one simple fabricated detail just to calm him.

"I didn't know I was pregnant," Mia blurted out.

Mia didn't want Lamont to know she neglected all of her morality for dick.

"You just found out," Lamont questioned instantly excited that the situation wasn't a total lost.

"Yea, I just found out yesterday," Mia fabricated. "I'm six weeks, Mia explained so that Lamont was well aware that Mia wasn't connecting Lamont to her new found pregnancy.

"Well what are you going to do, are you going to stay with him," Lamont asked.

"I don't know, I can't say that I'm 100 percent happy, so I'm just going to take it day by day for now," Mia confirmed as she connected with Lamont's eyes.

"Why Mia, how can a man fuck up with you," Lamont insisted as he grabbed her chin to lift her face from looking down.

Mia didn't want this conversation to get too far involved, but Mia could feel only butterflies as the conversation went on.

Even though Mia lied about unknowingly having sex while pregnant, Lamont completely understood and wanted nothing more than for Mia to be happy.

"He's too controlling Mont, I hate it. He tries to control me with everything. He tricked me into getting pregnant my lifestyle, school, everything.

Mia burst into tears. She genuinely hated the position she was in with Wayne, but a little acting to put herself back in Lamont's good graces wouldn't hurt.

"Oh baby, fuck that nigga, you don't deserve that," Lamont confirmed.

Lamont leaned into Mia and laid the softest kiss Mia has ever felt down on her lips. Mia decided to join Lamont in the kiss he started. Lamont found the bottom of Mia's dress and slid his hand up her thigh. He made his way to her passage and pointed his way through. Lamont pulled in and out as he watched Mia gasp for the breath she lost when her juices submerged Lamont's fingers.

Mia pulled back Lamont's hand.

"I can't do this again. Not like this. Let's link up, start fresh we can't do this," Justine advised as she remembered the wholesome girl Lamont left her as.

"You have to go, I'll call you when I leave," Mia encouraged as she pulled Lamont to my office door.

"Lamont didn't hesitate to leave he came and got exactly what he wanted. Lamont gained Mia's attention once again. Lamont left Pearl that night with a scent of Mia that would ignite his sensations his whole way home. Lamont was into Mia, and with or without baby, he seemed to be down for the ride.

"Damn, that man just does something to me," Mia stated as she watched my office door slam as she plopped down on the couch. Mia gathered her thoughts and decided to join the rest of the party. She scanned the room and nothing seemed out of the normal. Everything was pretty much the exact same way as it was when she left.

Our partygoers were in and dressing for their evenings out, while the rest of our guest mingled our sales floor admiring the pieces displayed for purchases. I sat back against the register pleased at how the evening turned out. Everyone seemed to be satisfied and I made quite the impression on the investors that had come. The evening came to an end as I watched our guests load up their vehicles with merchandise they had purchased that night.

"Honey, it's been a long night.  Ray and I will be staying at the Hyatt 3 blocks up if you need us. Good night honey, I enjoyed myself, you girls are doing an amazing job.  Baby call me in the morning so we can do breakfast. My mother explained as she made her way to the towne car waiting curbside for her.

"Yea, breakfast would be perfect, I have someone special I want you to meet, I'll bring him to breakfast," I stated to my mother as her eyes grew bigger.

I've never brought home a guy, so this was new to my mother's ears. I always kept my business under wraps; no one related to me knew anything of my love life.

"Wow, a man, whoa Dionne, this is news, we would love to meet him," My mother Eileen stated as she leaned in and kissed me on the cheek.

I said my goodbyes to them and walked over to Toney. My night had only begun.

"Hey babe, can you do breakfast in the morning with my parents," I asked Toney as he put his arms around my lower back kissing me on my forehead.

"Wow, breakfast with your parents, I would love to baby. Does that mean I get to stay the night," Toney insisted as he smiled as big as his cheeks would allow.

I could tell everyone was watching me across the room, but I didn't care, I had a fine man wrapped around me. They could all be jealous of me this time.

"Who the hell is this man Dionne has been all up under tonight," Mia asked as she looked at Dionne and Toney flirting with each other from across the room.

"Girl some man, she introduced me to when I first got here, we'll see if he stays, Dionne will be done with him in 48 hours," Tinsley stated blowing out candles illuminated on the tables.

"Well whoever he is, he is fine honey," Isaac added as he licked his lips.

"You so nasty," Mia confirmed as she spotted Justine walking over to them.

"Hey guys can we get rolling with the clean-up, we're trying to get out of here as soon as we can," Justine insisted as she picked up empty cups off of the table tops.

"Oh ok, sorry about that," Mia stated as she reached down to help Justine.

"Oh hell no, don't help that bitch do shit," Tinsley stated as she slapped the empty cup out of Mia's hand.

"Well damn, you so mean," Isaac stated as he laughed at Justine's reaction to what she just said.

There was nothing for Justine to say. It was no secret that Tinsley disliked her. Justine walked to the other side of the store and started cleaning up. Our last guest left the store at 1:40am. One of the hairstylist, make-up artist, Shayla, Jasmine and Valet team all left the party at 1:30am.

"Great turn out, right Dionne," Justine giggled from across the room, gathering flyers from the party tables.

"Yup a lot of people showed up, I stated as I looked around the empty store. All of the merchandise had been bought and the only thing we had left. was a few boxes in the back room.

I was more anxious to get to the bottom of all the bullshit that was festering in the store. I was not pleased, and I hated secrets amongst my staff. I ran a very successful business and no way was I about to let this situation bring us down.

"Let's see what we did tonight, he sold out of everything so I know we did well," Justine quoted as she walked toward the cash wrap to open the registers.

"Actually Justine I need to speak with you in my office, I stated as I turned to go back to my office.

"I'll just stay out here, let me know if you need me babe," Toney stated as he found a seat near the hairstyling stations.

"Babe, wait who are you," Mia stated as she sized Toney up and down.

"That's Toney Dionne's new boo, I met him earlier," Tinsley stated as she grabbed Toney's shoulder to confirm he was a good guy.

Tinsley knew exactly what was about to go down in the back office so back up was ready for action.

"Isaac, can you count us down while we wait, I'm trying to get the hell out of here, I'll help you," Tinsley stated as she delegated the register to Isaac, as Dionne had asked.

"Well yea, I guess we'll do that now," Isaac suggested, as he stood to his feet and headed to the register.

Tinsley realized that Dionne didn't have her phone with the only proof she had of Justine being a complete slut.

"Tinsley can you grab Wayne, Mia I need to speak with you as well," I stated peaking my head out onto the sales floor. Tinsley noticed Wayne pull around the front of the store with his car. Tinsley walked to the front door and called for him.

"Wayne, hey my sister would like to speak with you," Tinsley stated as Wayne put the car in park and left the hazard lights on.

Tinsley grabbed her phone from behind the cash wrap and walked Wayne back to Dionne's office.

"Oh damn, I thought the party was over, clearly it's just getting started," Isaac stated still sipping on Champaign and counting down the registers at the same time.

# Right under my nose

"I don't know what the hell is going on.  I called her phone five times," said Chewy the little brother of Justine. She said that the event would be over at 2am, and I still see cars parked outside.

"Do you know what car she drove up here," Chewy's friend Damon questioned as he rolled his lips around a Dutch cigarillo to seal the Kush in the blunt.

"No we're in the only car she owns, I have no idea if she's in there or not, let's just go across the street for drinks until she calls my phone.

Justine had done it again. She organized a robbery, right up under my nose. She picked the biggest night of business to plan for Pearl to be robbed. Only thing she didn't expect was to be caught up in a love triangle before she left for the night.

I had pulled all three of them in my office to get to the bottom of the madness. The only one who was owed an explanation was Mia.

Justine's brother Chewy and his friend Damon headed across the street to the Lucky bar for drinks until Justine gave them the green light.

"Listen Dionne I really don't know what this is about but I need to answer my phone," Justine confirmed as she searched her purse for her ringing phone.

"Yea Dionne what is this about, I'm ready to go, I'm getting sleepy," Mia agreed as Justine tried calling back Chewy's phone as she viewed his missed calls.

"Ok you're right so let's get down to the nitty gritty. Take a look at this," I encouraged as I handed Mia Tinsley's phone with the video of Justine and Wayne having sex on the conference table.

Wayne looked up at Mia as she watched the video still curious as to what she was watching.

"This you," Mia questioned as she turned Tinsley's phone toward him so he can view the same thing that she was seeing.

Wayne dropped his head into his hands. Mia handed the phone back to me and picked up the stapler off my desk and launched it at Wayne's head.

"Damn what the hell you throwing shit for," Wayne yelled as he watched Mia charge him and start swinging at his face.

"Mia calm down, I know you're pissed but you're pregnant," I shouted as Mia stopped hitting Wayne.

"And you Justine we're friends, why would you," Mia shouted at Justine as she pulled her phone away from her ear.

Just then Mia could hear the moans she was making in the conference room fill my office.

"Mia it wasn't supposed to happen like this, I was just a bit frustrated and Wayne was a listening shoulder once I returned back," Justine explained as she walked toward Mia.

"Don't you even touch me, you too are both some dumb fucks," Mia shouted as she burst out into tears.

"You know what maybe I was wrong for fucking Justine today, but you were in Chicago with other men, you forgot to mention that huh Mia," Wayne shouted exposing the fact that he knew Mia had been unfaithful as well.

"Yea Justine, told be all about your little trip with some guy, while you're carrying my child. How else do you think I'm supposed to accept that type of shit? I walked in hear wanting to apologize for not considering your feelings about the pregnancy and you were out not giving a fuck about mine," Wayne defended.

"Wait I only told you she was in Chicago, I never told you she was with another guy," Justine fabricated trying to cover up her deceit.

"Cut the shit Justine you told me everything, stop insulting her intelligence she knows what happened it's no need to continue to lie," Wayne insisted as he stood to face the door.

"Listen Mia, I fucked up, but I've been running off of emotions for 4 days. You're running from me, I don't know what's going on with us, let's resolve this once and for all, and I won't be upset if you don't want anything to do with me," Wayne declared.

Wayne had somehow flipped this whole thing on Mia, I had enough of the bull shit.

"Wayne No, you can't possibly think that by having Justine on the conference table, can be patched up with only saying you're sorry," I explained as I denied the fact that Mia played a part in the drama.

"It's a start Dionne, and that's all we have left," Wayne responded as he stood to his feet to help Mia out of her seat. He had been parking cars all night and hadn't seen Mia in four days.

"Fine, let me grab my things," Mia stated.

Mia knew that she held some responsibility. She thought back to her visit tonight and her creeping in Chicago and decided to focus on how she truly felt and if she even wanted to continue a relationship with Wayne. She had a lot going on and needed to call it a night before someone got hurt. Mia knew that Wayne worshiped the ground she walked on and was only acting out because she was ignoring him; she was willing to compromise on behalf of her being pregnant. Mia and Wayne walked toward the door of Dionne's office. First Wayne and Mia following.

"It's a damn shame you can be so phony Justine, you sit in my face day after day listening to my problems to fuck my man in the conference room, how you feel. Can't feel too good because you're trifling ass is still going home alone," Mia shouted as she walked out of the door.

Tinsley, Isaac and Toney looked up as they watched Mia and Wayne leave the boutique.

"Damn, what did I miss," Questioned Isaac as he finished up counting the money from tonight's sales.

"Justine, could you shut my door please," I asked as Justine stood near the door scrolling through her phone.

"So clearly you understand you have gone against company policy? After watching the video I can really file a suit against you, you do know that right Justine," I asked as Justine focused her attention on her phone. She had no interest to save her name. She didn't care that the video was playing or the fact that she had just lost her job. She gave no fucks, that evening.

"But I'm not going to do that, I'm simply going to let you go," I confirmed as I watched Justine grow infuriated with my decision I had just made.

"I don't have the time or the patience to deal with you in court,"

"Yea, well you know you'd lose," Justine interrupted.

"Win or lose I don't want to see your face after today, I want you to leave, turn in all keys and access you have to the boutique," I continued.

"You know what Dionne, I've done too much for this company for you to let me go because of one mistake.  There is plenty of illegal shit that goes on here and I'm being let go," Justine argued as she walked toward the door.

"You're right there is a lot of shit going on right up under my nose. Shit that some of you have gotten away with for so long. I'm putting a stop to it tonight. You are no longer an employee of Pearl," I advised as I walked to the door to let Justine out.

I had enough, the bitch had to be out of her mind to think she would stay after finding something like this out. How the hell could she ever be trusted again? I walked out of my office and could see Justine walking across the street to Lucky's bar.

"Justine is no longer working with us. She has gotten fired, as I informed my remaining staff.

"What did I miss, Isaac stated as he handed me over the deposit bags and money box to take back to the safe.

"Justine was having sex with Wayne while you guys were getting dressed for tonight, in the conference room," I advised.

"What, are you serious, that skank," Isaac proclaimed.

"Yea, that's what happens when you put your faith in uppity bitches, they think they run the place," Tinsley stated out of jealousy. Tinsley had been looked over because of Justine for so long. This time Tinsley had the opportunity to make it right with Pearl.

"Can you guys handle closing tonight," I asked as a sat down on Toney's lap exhausted.

"Yea we can handle it. We're locking up the money and then locking up, we got it under control," Isaac confirmed as he walked toward my office.

"Babe, you ready to go, I'm leaving my car here, and I'll get it in the morning. It's parked around back. Can you drive to my place," I asked Toney as I walked to my office for my purse.

"Of Course, let's go baby, it's been a long day for you," Toney suggested as he grabbed our bags out of my hands and lead the way out of the front door.

"Goodnight Dionne, Goodnight Toney, "Tinsley stated as she held the door open for us to lock it after we left.

"Good night call me in the morning, don't forget breakfast in the morning with mom and Mr. Ray," I reminded Tinsley.

"Where are you staying tonight," I asked, noticing that Tinsley had been staying over my apartment these last few days.

"I'm staying at the Hyatt where mom and Mr. Ray are tonight. Need some alone time," Tinsley suggested.

"Ok sister, thank you so much for keeping everything in line today. I couldn't have done it without you, don't forget to call Mia for breakfast in the morning" I advised Tinsley.

I left the boutique with Toney that night. I was very exhausted and ready to snuggle up with my newfound love. I fired Justine, but immediately after the words slipped my mouth, I felt relieved. I knew that Mia would more than likely forgive Wayne for cheating on her, because he had found out that she had been unfaithful in Chicago.

"You ready to go, Isaac," Tinsley asked Isaac as they shut off the store lights.

"Yea, let's go.  Did you want to go across the street to get a quick drink," Isaac asked as Tinsley and Isaac walked out of the back door and locked up the store.

"I can't believe your sister fired Justine," Isaac added.

"Yea well you do fucked up shit, fucked up shit will happen to you, Tinsley proclaimed as she put her bags in the trunk.

"Yea, but damn, why Mia though. Who does she think she is, that's some selfish shit to do to someone you call a friend," Isaac confirmed.

Tinsley and Isaac went across the street to the Lucky's bar to get a drink. As soon as they stepped inside they watched Justine telling two men the story on how she was fired from a shitty boutique across the street.

"Why is this bitch in here," Tinsley questioned grabbing a seat at the bar.

"It's going to be problems if she even looks this direction," Isaac stated.

Isaac ordered double shots of Hennessey for the both of them. The two men Justine was talking with suddenly left in a hurry. Justine sat at the bar and finished her drinks.

"Yea something just doesn't seem right, why is this bitch sitting at the bar, where is her car, because she walked out of the front door and I don't remember seeing her get in the car," Tinsley stated confused.

"Yea, I'm not sure, all I know is I'm going home to my boo, I have had my fair share of drama for the day, Justine doesn't want problems, let her soak up in her emotions, she was fired today, and lost a good friend, let her drink," Isaac decreed.

Tinsley and Isaac left the bar after finishing their first drink. They saw Justine notice them leaving. Tinsley decided to give Justine the dirtiest look she had ever seen. Flicking her off as she put on her jacket.

Tinsley and Isaac walked back across the street to their cars.

"Alright, I'm out I need to get some rest, Thanks for the drink," Tinsley called out to Isaac.

"No problem, I'll see you Monday boo be careful," Isaac responded.

Tinsley drove off as Isaac unlocked his car door. Isaac opened his car door and felt a huge blow to the back of his head. Isaac hit the ground and felt for blood. He immediately felt his face stinging. He could feel wet boots kicking him in his side and in his face. Two men had nearly beaten Isaac to death. As cars drove past, the two men panicked and couldn't finish the job. They got into a car similar to Justine's black Audi and sped away.

# Man Down

"Hi is this Dionne," A man over the phone questioned.

"Yes, this is she, may I ask who's calling" Dionne spoke as she tried to adjust her eyes to wake up.

"Yes we found a man outside of the door of your store, also there was a break in and vandalism to the front of the store, would you mind coming into the station for questioning," the police officer spoke over the phone.

"Can I stop by my store first, I need to verify what's been stolen so I can contact the insurance company," Dionne questioned as she put her shoes on.

"Yes you can stop by, there is an officer there, you would want to tell him that you've already spoken to me and will be at the station afterwards.

"This is some bullshit, somebody broke into the store," I shouted as I flipped on the lights in my bedroom.

"What, I'm coming with you," Toney confirmed as he stood to his feet to put on his clothes.

We drove a block down the street and witnessed 4 cop cars and an ambulance in the middle of the street. As Toney parked the car, I jumped out of the passenger screaming for Isaac.

"Hey officer, is he okay," I shouted as I watched the EMS tech's lift Isaac on the gurney.

"Can I see him," I shouted as I grabbed the tech's jacket.

"Hello, this is my shop he works here," I advised.

The tech let me into the truck as the other techs covered Isaac's face with an oxygen mask.

"Hey boo, are you ok," I said to Isaac as I watched him struggle to breathe.

"Dionne, don't worry about me, I'll be fine, they took the money Dionne, and they were driving a car just like Justine's. Same color, same style," Isaac confirmed as the tech located a few broken ribs.

"Ok, we're going to find out who did this to you," I confirmed.

I was pissed. After all that had been going on, this by far was the worst. I already got a heads up that the safe in my office had been cracked open. I didn't want to go inside to see what had all been vandalized. The insurance company had informed me to call the contractor for temporary repairs.

"I hope Isaac is ok, I can't believe this happened to him. I hope we find out who did this today," I advised Toney frantic as I wondered how this could have happened right under my nose.

"Babe we'll find out who did this," Toney advised as he rubbed my back with his right hand while steering with his left.

We arrived at the police station as the police had instructed. Toney advised that he would stay in the car so he could make a few phones calls to friends of his who owns bars near the store. He wanted to check with them to see if anyone had witnessed anything.

"Hello, My name is Dionne, I'm here for questioning, my boutique was robbed and…" Before I could finish explaining to the officer at the desk why I was at the station he redirected me to the office right across the hall.

"You can go right on in and have a seat, Officer Delaney will be right with you," The officer sitting at the receptionist desk advised.

"Within' hours of me firing Justine, my store is vandalized and robbed. I needed to find out if Tinsley and Isaac secured the safe and the doors at the store. We had surveillance cameras set up in and around the store. I knew we could get something off of it.

"Hello, Dionne, I'm Officer Delaney," Said a tall brown man with bulging muscles bursting out of his shirt.

"Hello, how are you," I asked Officer Delaney.

"I'm good, thanks. So, we responded to a 911 call earlier this morning around 4am. The caller reported hearing glass shattering and a man screaming shortly after," Explained Officer Delaney.

"Ms. Elwood, where were you at 4a.m this morning," Officer Delaney questioned.

"I was sleep, in my bed. Where I was when you called," I responded.

"I'm only asking because witnesses told us that they seen you leave your store in the early morning hours..." Officer Delaney advised as I interrupted.

"We had an event last night, that ended about 1am and of course I had to close my store," I snapped.

"Oh, ok no problem, I just need to make sure we have this documented," Officer Delaney confirmed.

"We actually found the robbers responsible three miles away from the store," Officer Delaney advised.

"We found a car the same make and model that the victim of the brutal beating claimed had drove away after he was beaten. We were able to retrieve $21,000 cash from the vehicle. If you are able to prove this was the money from the store you can have the money back," Officer Delaney advised.

"Ok, no problem, I'll bring you my media reports from the register in an hour," I advised as I stood to my feet to leave Officer Delaney's office.

"I will be in touch, Dionne, I also have to go to the hospital where the victim is and speak to him regarding the men that were arrested. If you can bring me back your reports from the store then we have them, I can convict them of the crime," Officer Delaney advised.

"Will do, I have your number and I will get those reports to right away," I agreed as I walked out of Officer Delany's office and outside to Toney's car where he was waiting for me.

I was unsure of the cash amount that was in the safe, but I was most certain that wouldn't be a problem proving that this was the money from the safe. One thing Justine was good for was supplying us with resources to secure and count funds that came through the store.

I checked my phone and noticed my mother and step father had been calling all morning, I knew Tinsley or Mia had been in contact with them because I sent both of them text messages to let them know that Isaac had gotten beaten up last night after the party.

"Babe I know you got a lot going on so I took care of the contractor, he's already made it out to Pearl and replacing the window and back door, Tinsley, Mia and your mom is there now," Toney stated as he pulled out of the driveway of the police station.

I think I fell in love with Toney that day. His determination and willingness to help me made me want to submit myself to him.  I was overwhelmed with everything that was happening to my sisters and I. As Toney voiced his opinions about the past twenty-four hours, I became lost in his words. I looked at his lips mesmerized at the good man I had sitting before me. I dropped my head into Toney's lap and pulled his manhood out of his pants. I put Toney's rod in my mouth and soaked his shaft with my tongue. I began stroking

Toney as he squirmed in the driver's seat. Toney pulled up in a

nearby parking lot and indulged in the head he was receiving

while driving. As the moans echoed the inside of the car I

stroked and stroked as Toney ejaculated into my mouth.

"Damn Babe, where did that come from," Toney

questioned as he looked down at an expected mess, realizing I

didn't leave a drop.

I leaned out of the passenger door spitting out the cum

that Toney had shot into my mouth.

"Babe, I get so horny when I see you taking control.

These last few days, you have made these hard moments so

much easier.  It's like things are getting done. My staff respects

you," I advised Toney as I watched a smile appear on his face.

"Yea, and You know why, because they respect you, I got

you boo, I've noticed your strength far before you let me this

close to you. I am committed to this, and I won't leave your side," Toney proclaimed as he grabbed my hand resting on the gearshift.

"Thank you Honey, you are amazing. I'm ready to get pass this. It has to be someone close to me, they robbed me right under my nose," I stated as I leaned back into the passenger seat.

Toney and I hurried back to the store so I could get the media reports to prove the money retrieved from the vehicle belonged to Pearl.

# UP TO ME

Two weeks had passed and Pearl was running as normal. The police returned the stolen money and Isaac was discharged from the hospital.

"Well Sis, we back, just like we never left," Tinsley shouted from the storefront window, as she dressed the mannequins.

"Minor setback, for a major come back," I chuckled as I finished up with paper work behind the cash wrap.

"Speaking of that, how are you and Pierre, Mr. Grand," I questioned jokingly.

I noticed Pierre hasn't been the topic of discussion in a while and Tinsley seemed relieved.

"Uhm, well I'm done with Pierre's ass. I went to the clinic a few day ago, and apparently the nigga gave me chlamydia," Tinsley confessed as she walked toward me standing at the cash wrap.

"Oh hell no, fuck him, Tinsley you need to really be done, then Isaac's friend Ryan having information on him, he proly fuckin' with a gay man on the low, leave his ass alone Tinsley I'm serious," I lectured.

I prayed to God Tinsley was serious I was tired of that cornball ass niggas walking all over my sister. I wanted to be more of an example for my sisters. I noticed that they looked up to me. My opinion mattered to them and the best thing I could give is guidance.

"Yea, I'm done. I'm definitely not mad. I continued to fuck with him even after I knew he was fucking with other females. I blame myself. I decided to forgive him and move on with life. I can't hold on to the hurt forever. As long as I'm upset that Pierre fucked me over so many times, he'll control me, and I'm sick of that.  I'm tired of giving him the power to control me," Tinsley explained.

For the first time in life I truly believed Tinsley was really done with Pierre.

I decided I should be more hands-on in the boutique. Even though I let Justine go, she was an amazing asset to my team, and I wasn't quite sure I would find someone that would do as good as job as she did.

"Hey Ladies did you miss me.  I got some news for you heifers, yal need to sit down for this one," Isaac shouted as he entered the boutique.

"Oh hey Bitch," I shouted as I noticed my friend Isaac alive and well walking into our store.

"Look at you, you look good baby," I added as I grabbed Isaac in for a kiss.

"Thank You Honey, Thank You," Isaac stated as he checked himself out.

Isaac noticed Tinsley sitting in the chair in front of him teary eyed.

"Hey baby bop," Isaac stated jokingly trying to break the ice of the bitter yet sweet moment that existed on the sales floor.

"Hey Ike, I just can't believe I was right there, I could've helped, Why didn't I stay. Where were they when I was getting in my car? Why didn't I notice them," Tinsley cried out.

"Hey, Hey It's okay. What if you were there when it happened? Something may have happened to you Tinsley. Don't blame yourself those idiots," Isaac assured as he wiped Tinsley's tears.

"I know I just wish," Tinsley started as Isaac interrupted.

"You wish nothing. Everything happens for a reason. Besides if you were there I may have not been able to tell yal the latest," Isaac informed as he placed his bags down and grabbed a seat next to the ladies.

"What the hell is going on," I stated as I crossed my legs seated in the royalty chairs on the sales floor.

"So you know, I had court this morning. They are dropping the charges to assault and battery rather than

attempted murder," so I'm feeling a little on edge about it,"
Isaac alerted.

"They broke three of your ribs and pistol-whipped you, I
don't understand how they feel those men weren't trying to kill
you," I stated infuriated.

"Yea, well that was his argument, his lawyer is saying
this wasn't attempted murder because, he did have a gun and
did not shoot, he used his gun to inflict bodily harm instead so,
they're more than likely going to drop it to assault and battery,
Isaac explained.

"Listen that's not what I had to tell you, so Ryan picked
me up from court and guess who picked up the motherfucker
who did this, Isaac asked as Tinsley and I looked at him waiting
on the answer.

"Who," Tinsley and I recited in unison.

"Justine," Isaac responded.

"I knew it, I fucking knew it. That bitch," I shouted, as I
looked at Tinsley with her mouth stuck wide open.

"But hold on, there's more, I saw his statement after court, he's saying Pierre paid him and gave him the name and description of a man to beat up," Isaac continued.

"So he snitched on Pierre," Tinsley questioned, in genuine concern for her ex-boyfriend.

"Fuck him," Isaac stated in a harsh tone.

"Wait what is the guy's name who did this to you," I asked.

Justine was a close friend of mine, anyone she knew I pretty much knew.

Well you know it was two of them, James Howard and Lance Malloy," Isaac advised.

"Shut the fuck up, that's Justine's little brother, I added.

"Yea Lance Malloy who goes by Chewy, is Justine's little brother," I confirmed.

"See that bitch got me fucked up, you know what I got something for her ass," I stated pissed that I had a dirty snake ass bitch that close to my funds. No telling what the hell she had up her sleeve. I instantly felt trapped. I thought of every single financial transaction that Justine had ever done for my business. People that recognize her at the bank. Hell people she may know at the bank who were willing to do favors. I couldn't breathe I suddenly got sick of the thought of all the malicious ways Justine could've been plotting to take me down.

At that very moment I decided to pay Justine a visit. I wanted to know beforehand. I had to find out what the hell was on her mind. She was responsible for all this bullshit. There was no way in hell I'd let this bitter bitch come up into my territory and pull a fast one on me right in front of my face. I was more than willing to help anyone when it came to finances. I sponsored trips; my staff even received commission and bonuses. But see that money was too good. Bitches became spoiled. The money they were making from bonuses and commission was more than their hourly salary, but that wasn't enough. They wanted more. They wanted mine, and that shit, had to cease.  I listened as Isaac finished telling us his story about court. I figured it was better no one knew what the hell I

was up to.

# NO SUCH THING AS A DEAD BEAT MOTHER

"I was expecting you to be there, I paid for your flight and you never showed," Mia stated on the phone to her mother.

Mia kept a lot of her emotions to herself she's lived with us since she was 3. Her mother lived in Texas. Mia's mom has never been to Ohio to see Mia. Mia always made trips to Texas to visit her mother. She yearned for a normal mother daughter relationship with her mother, but it was like the more she tried, the more her mother resisted.

"I couldn't take the time off from work Mia, I'm sorry." Mia's mother Michelle confirmed.

"Ok, I'll talk to you later mom, Mia stated as she rushed her mother off of the phone.

"I just don't understand, why is my mom so nonchalant. She doesn't give a damn about how I feel. It's like she's perfectly fine with another woman stepping in taking her place, and don't get me wrong, Mrs. Eileen means the world to me, but damn, I feel like I'm not good enough to my own mother," Mia explained as tears filled her eyes.

"Mia you're pregnant now, you can't stress over small things anymore. Why don't you just go down there, take Wayne, you guys are trying to repair your relationship and he's never met your mom, this would be a really good time to take a trip," I advised Mia as she curled up on my couch.

"I think you're right. I'll talk to Wayne and see what he wants to do, I just don't want to start to hate my mother. I'm about to bring a child into this world, I would resent my mother if she neglects to have some type of relationship with her grandchild I'd hate her forever," Mia explained.

I felt so horrible for my baby sister. Mia had a different mother than Tinsley and I, but her hurt was our hurt. I hated to see her going through this. Especially when I knew there was nothing I could do.

That following week Mia booked a flight to Austin, Texas to visit her mother. Wayne agreed to accompany her.

"Well, damn they only reason I get to meet your mom is because you're pregnant," Wayne antagonized.

"Please don't start, we are also supposed to be working on us, and you're already pissing me off," Mia informed as her and Wayne boarded the plane.

Mia was anxious to get to her mother's house.  She wasn't even up in the air before Wayne started stressing her about irrelevant shit. He knew Mia didn't have a good relationship with her mother. Mia secluded herself the remainder of the trip. On the inside she was still hurt that Wayne had been unfaithful. She knew she couldn't say a word to Wayne about how she was feeling, because he would throw the fact that she cheated while pregnant. Mia and Wayne landed in Texas and called a cab to drive them to her mother's house.

"Did you call your mom to tell her we were on the way," Wayne questioned as he grabbed his and Mia's luggage from baggage claim.

"No, we're just going to pop up, hopefully she's home, if not we'll try again tomorrow," Mia confirmed.

Mia was afraid that if she notified her mom of her arrival, she would stand her up.

Mia and Wayne pulled up to Mia's mother's house. Mia noticed the garage door open and two cars parked in the driveway. Mia and Wayne paid the cab driver and walked to the front door.

"Ok Wayne, try not to be so condescending around my mother. I know you don't care too much for her, but she's still my mother," Mia instructed as she rang the doorbell.

"She better not say anything stupid and we won't..."

Just then the front door flew open. A tall man with black hair and a grey beard answered the stood at the front door. He wore a chief's apron and held meat tongs in his hands.

"Hello, how can I help you," The man asked as he stood in the doorway.

"Uhm yes I'm Mia, Michelle Wright's daughter," Mia responded.

The man at the door dropped the tongs in his hands and screamed for Michelle.

"Michelle get down here," The man shouted.

Just then Mia's mom appeared at the front door holding a baby.

"Mia, what are you doing here, I had no idea you were coming," Michelle proclaimed.

"Yea well, this is my boyfriend Wayne and we're here in town visiting his parents, I figured we'd stop by on the way," Mia fabricated.

Wayne knew his parents were in Columbus, Ohio however he decided to follow Mia's story and take her lead.

"Come in, Come in," The man offered.

"Are you guys hungry, I just put some burgers on the grill, you guys are more than welcome to join us out back," The man stated.

"I'm Michael, your mother's husband.  This is Brielle, our daughter, your little sister, she actually just had her first birthday 2 weeks ago," Michael advised.

Mia instantly felt cold. She was watching her mother parent a baby. She doesn't have many memories with her mother when she was young. Her baby sister was so beautiful, she was a tad bit darker than Mia, but she had big brown eyes, and a huge curly Afro slicked back by a headband. Mia didn't know how to react to her mother having a baby and not telling Mia. At that very moment Mia decided to turn each negative situation, she felt her mother had thrown at her into a positive one.

Mia felt Michael's hospitality and immediately felt comfortable enough to take off her shoes and stay for something to eat, however she felt a slight distance coming from her mother. Her husband was so open to her popping up.

"I don't mind joining you guys for dinner," Mia stated.

Mia, Wayne, Michael and Michelle walked to the back patio where the aroma of turkey burgers clouded the air.

Mia had no idea her mother had a baby. It's been well over a year since she last saw her mother but they talked often enough for her to mention she had a little sister.

Mia kept looking at baby Brielle, and wanted to hold her.

"Can I hold her, Mia requested as she extended her arms to reach for her baby sister?

"Brielle reached out for Mia at almost the same moment. Brielle leaped out Michelle's lap and wrapped her arms around Mia's next.

"Oh look at that. Stated Michael as he smiled and chuckled at Brielle playing with Mia's earrings.

Brielle sat in Mia's lap five minutes before she bursts into tears and squirmed to get down. Mia recognized that Brielle may have sensed another baby and gave her back to her mother.

"Aww she must be sleepy, I'll go lay her down," Michelle confirmed as she walked back into the house with Brielle.

"So Wayne what area of town do your parents live," Michael insisted as he took a seat at the bistro table on the patio deck.

Mia interrupted with a response because she knew it was her lie that landed them on the back porch for dinner in the first place.

"They're actually driving in from out of town to meet us and then we're going to follow them home, they just moved here," Mia fabricated.

"Oh ok, well that works out," Michael added.

Michael and Wayne continued on about the basketball tournaments. Mia zoned completely out and envisioned her mother holding her baby sister. Mia knew at that very moment that Michelle wouldn't have any type of interest of being a grandmother to Mia's unborn. Mia decided to join her mother in the house to give her the latest updates about her life.

Mia left Michael and Wayne to finish their conversation on the back patio. She found her mother in the living room laying baby Brielle down in her play pin.

"Hey mom," Mia called out as Michelle noticed Mia standing above her.

"Hey Mia, Brielle was really tired, she hadn't had a nap all day," Michelle continued as she took a seat across from Mia.

"Mom why didn't you tell me I had a little sister," Mia questioned in complete astonishment that her mother would leave out such an important detail. Mia had already felt the distance between her and her mother, but seeing her mother another child she had no idea about confirmed that Michelle was not interested in including Mia in her life.

"Well Mia, I knew you were busy with your business and school, I didn't want to worry you with what I had going on," Michelle confirmed.

"Mom, a baby sister would never worry me. If anything I'd be excited," Mia concluded as she crossed her arms and looked in the direction of Brielle sleeping in her play pin.

"I had a very complicated pregnancy, I didn't even know if I'd make it out alive. I should've sent pictures but it kind of went by so fast," Michelle defended.

Mia decided to leave the conversation right there. She couldn't argue with her mother's decision not to include her on the arrival of her baby sister. Mia knew what type of mother she wanted to be, and she wasn't at all ready to bear a child. She was upset at the fact that it was happening before her planned time, but she embraced it. She put herself in a mothers mind set immediately after she decided she was bringing a child into the world.  Mr. Ray told Mia that he and Michelle planned Mia. They wanted a baby girl and they received her.

Mia decided to give her mother the latest of her life. She confided in Eileen for advice, but didn't want to disappoint her father. She felt like herself around her mother. No matter how long they went without speaking. She always felt her mother didn't judge her for bad decisions that she may have made.

"Mom I'm pregnant," Mia blurted out.

Mia decided to be the bigger person and include her mother on her pregnancy. It took every piece of strength for her to do the right thing. She decided to let her mother make her own bad decisions. If Michelle didn't want to be a part of her grandchild's life, Mia wasn't going to force her.

"Babe you read to go," Wayne called out as he entered the house through the back door with Michael.

Wayne came in the house just in time. Mia handed her mother the information that would make or break the rest of their relationship. Mia didn't have any more energy to give to her and her mother's relationship. She was about to bring a child into the world.  Everything that she had, needed to go toward her unborn.

Mia stood to her feet and gave her mother a hug. Michael walked over and gave Mia a hug and kiss on the forehead.

"I hate that you guys have to go so soon, maybe you guys can stop back through before you head back home," Michael suggested as he walked Mia and Wayne to the front door.

Mia looked back at baby Brielle and spotted her mother picking her up out of the play pin. She glimpsed at her mother cuddling Brielle and kissing on her while sleep.

"Nice meeting you Wayne, you guys be safe," Michael added as he shut the door.

Wayne had contacted a cab and decided to get Mia home as fast as possible. He could tell that she was on edge after noticing she had a baby sister she knew nothing of.

"Well that was an interesting visit," Wayne stated.

"Yea," Mia answered short and dry looking at the front of the house, becoming obsessed with wanting a family of her own.

"Babe you all right," Wayne questioned as he noticed Mia gazing out of the car window.

"I just don't get it Wayne," Mia proclaimed as she tried to make sense of the not so existent relationship that existed between her and her mother.

"I mean our child may not know my mother," Mia confirmed.

"Yea, but she has Mrs. Eileen, Mr. Ray and my parents," Wayne Confirmed as he rubbed Mia's back.

"Yea, but," Mia stated unsure of her next word.

"It'll be okay Mia, it's your mothers lost, not yours. You are amazing Mia, and I'm sorry I gave you such a hard time about having my baby. It's your body and you shouldn't feel rushed or forced to do something you don't want to do. I guess

I got a little selfish. I wanted you all to myself, I'm so terrified I'll lose you," Wayne stated as he pulled Mia in closer to him.

Mia and Wayne were so close; they were best friends and depended on each other for everything. Mia decided to move forward with Wayne, after all when things were good they were good, and besides photo shop and airbrush would hide the things pregnancy may destroy. Why not enjoy both worlds.

Mia and Wayne arrived at a hotel near the airport. They knew they would be going home in the next 48 hours and wanted to get some rest.

"Hey babe, go on ahead up to the room, I'm going to the pool for a second, I want to talk to Dionne check in and make sure everything is ok," Mia suggested to Wayne as Wayne grabbed the hotel room keys from the administrator at the check in counter.

"Ok babe see you in the room," Wayne proclaimed as he walked toward the elevator.

Mia made her way to the lobby couch and dialed my phone.

"Hey sister, what are you up to," Mia stated.

"Nothing girl at the boutique getting some things done, what's up," I questioned, anxious to hear about Mia's visit with her mother.

"Girl I don't know, I told my mom everything that was going on with me, she really didn't seem too concerned Dionne," Mia stated.

"Well Boo, you made the effort, that's all you can put down, she's the mother and you're the child, if she can't give you guidance as a mother, than you should lead by example. You will be a fantastic mother to your baby. She'll only have to respect you after that," I encouraged. Mia seemed down and I didn't like her tone. My mother has always been there for me, so I couldn't imagine feeling what Mia felt.

Mia and I chatted on the phone for about an hour. She advised me about her connection with Wayne in the cab and how she wanted to give a second chance. She told me that she

arrived at her mother's house and found out she had a baby

sister. She owed it to herself to be the mother Michelle never

was to her.

# MY BABY

"Hello Mrs. Carlson, this is Veronica Fields," The voice over the phone confirmed.

"Yes, this is she," Eileen confirmed

"We have your daughter Dionne in our IC unit about to undergo surgery, she was involved in a fatal car accident earlier tonight. She was unconscious when the medics arrived.

The phone that Eileen was speaking on hit the floor.

"Oh my goodness Ray get up, get up, we have to go the hospital, its Dionne she's been in an accident, call the girls," Eileen suggested as she ran to the closet for clothes.

Eileen rushed to the downtown hospital unsure of the news she would receive once she arrived.

I received the emergency phone calls and made my way to the hospital. Upon my arrival I noticed everyone sitting in the lobby. I decided to sneak past them and see Dionne first. I walked into Dionne's room in the IC unit and noticed Eileen sitting in the chair next to Dionne reading her journal.

"Oh hey, how is she," I asked. I could notice Dionne's body swollen. She was almost unrecognizable. I swallowed the huge gulp in my throat and leaned against the counter on the other side of the room.

"Did you know about this," Eileen questioned as she held Dionne's journal up in the air so U could see.

"No, what is it," I questioned confused at what the black book entailed.

"Dionne has been keeping a journal these last few months," Eileen confirmed.

"Oh wow, no I had no idea," I assured.

"There is a lot of descriptive detail in it," Eileen confirmed.

Eileen seemed to be a bit bothered at what she read in Dionne's journal. I had no idea Dionne even liked to write.

"She was writing a book, and I think she was almost finished," Eileen added.

"Dionne lost a lot of blood and oxygen to the brain, what if," Eileen started to sob using Dionne's journal as a shield to hide her streaming tears.

"Dionne will be fine, she will be ok, I confirmed.

Even after seeing Dionne in the worst state of her life, I could see life all over Dionne, not death. She was going to pull through. I walked over toward Eileen and kneeled down to hug her.

"She'll be fine, I promise," I stated to Eileen as she looked up at Dionne laying in the hospital bed.

"I want to have her book published. I want to finish it. I want to write the ending," Eileen listed as she wiped her face.

"Will you help me, you seem to be very close to her and I know Dionne would be pleased, look she has a title and chapters, she was writing a book. Eileen persuaded.

"I will help you I confirmed. I couldn't go against Dionne's mother, besides if I knew Dionne like I know Dionne, she's all about making money.

"Thank you, I know she'll be pleased.

Eileen looked back at Dionne and caressed her arm.

"Dionne, mommy's here, I love you baby," Eileen spoke to Dionne as she laid there unconscious.

"Mia, you're pregnant," Eileen interrogated.